Nancy Drew
in
The Ringmaster's Secret

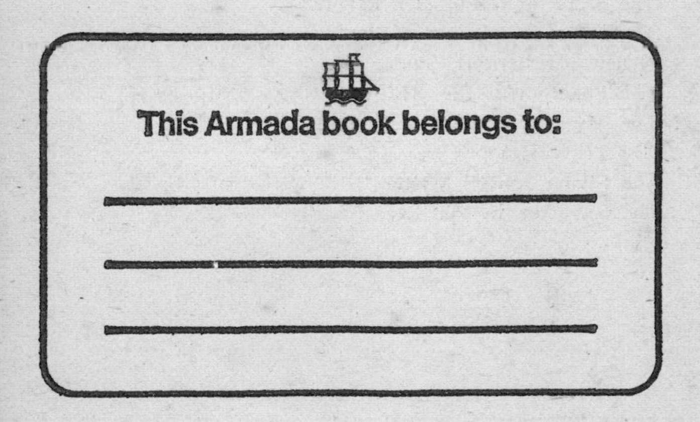

Other Nancy Drew Mystery Stories in Armada

The Secret of Shadow Ranch
The Mystery of the 99 Steps
Mystery at the Ski Jump
The Spider Sapphire Mystery
The Clue in the Crossword Cipher
The Quest of the Missing Map
The Clue in the Old Stagecoach
The Clue of the Broken Locket
The Message in the Hollow Oak
The Invisible Intruder
The Ghost of Blackwood Hall
Password to Larkspur Lane
The Bungalow Mystery
The Whispering Statue
The Haunted Showboat
The Clue of the Dancing Puppet
The Clue of the Tapping Heels
The Clue in the Crumbling Wall
The Mystery of the Tolling Bell
The Clue of the Black Keys
The Clue of the Leaning Chimney
The Scarlet Slipper Mystery
The Secret of the Golden Pavilion
The Secret in the Old Attic
Nancy's Mysterious Letter
The Phantom of Pine Hill
The Mystery of the Fire Dragon
The Triple Hoax
The Flying Saucer Mystery
The Secret in the Old Lace

The Nancy Drew Mystery Stories

The Ringmaster's Secret

Carolyn Keene

First published in the U.K. in 1973 by
William Collins Sons & Co. Ltd., London and Glasgow.
First published in Armada in 1981 by
Fontana Paperbacks,
14 St. James's Place, London SW1A 1PS.

This impression 1982.

Printed in Great Britain by
Love & Malcomson Ltd., Brighton Road,
Redhill, Surrey.

CONTENTS

Nancy quickly scribbled a note to Pietro.

·1·

The Golden Charms

"OH, Nancy, I worry so about your doing that trick riding," remarked Hannah Gruen, the Drews' house-keeper, looking fondly at the slender, attractive girl in jodhpurs and tight-fitting coat.

Eighteen-year-old Nancy Drew was about to leave the house for a morning riding lesson. She had paused to look at the mail on the hall table.

Putting an arm affectionately about plump Mrs Gruen, who had acted as mother to her since Mrs Drew's death many years before, Nancy added with a smile:

"If you're worrying about my safety, I haven't had a spill in months. Señor Roberto is too good a teach— Why, look!" she interrupted herself. "Here's a letter and the mystery package from New York!"

"What do you mean, Nancy?"

"Didn't I tell you, Hannah? Aunt Eloise sent a card saying she was sending me a gift that has an unusual story."

Nancy opened the letter from her aunt and began to read part of it aloud:

"—and the shopkeeper, who purchased it while on a buying trip in Europe, said it had been presented to a woman circus performer by a queen who loved horses. For some unknown reason the performer had to sell it but would not reveal her true identity. According to the story, however, she needs help badly—"

As Nancy paused, Hannah Gruen remarked with a sigh, "And I suppose that you're going to try to find this circus performer and help her out of her troubles. That's what you always do. Well, open the box and let's see what the mysterious gift is."

Nancy unwrapped several layers of tissue paper before she came to Aunt Eloise's present. Then, holding up an exquisite gold bracelet, she exclaimed:

"Look at all those darling little horse charms on it! One, two, three, four, five of them! Oh, oh, a sixth one is missing."

"It doesn't matter," said Hannah. "The bracelet's beautiful enough without the other horse."

Nancy slipped the dainty bracelet over her wrist and held up her arm to look at the effect. The tiny horses gleamed in the light and seemed almost alive, they were so perfectly wrought. Each displayed a different gait, and all were gracefully poised.

The girl's blue eyes suddenly sparkled and she snapped her fingers. "I can start sleuthing right away by asking Señor Roberto some questions. You know, he used to be with Sims' Circus."

"Yes, and I wish he'd never left it and opened that riding academy here in River Heights," Hannah declared. "Then you wouldn't have learned how to ride without a saddle and jump on to a moving horse and—"

Nancy laughed. "It's fun. And by the way, did you know Sims' Circus is coming to town tomorrow?"

"You bet it is," said a young voice from the back of the hall.

The others turned to see six-year-old Teddy Brown,

a neighbour, who had come in the back way. The red-haired, freckle-faced boy was grinning broadly.

"And don't forget, Nancy," he went on, "you promised to take me to see the circus men put up the tents and everything."

"That's right, Teddy. We'll leave your house at five o'clock tomorrow morning." Nancy tweaked his nose affectionately. "That's very early. Sure you'll be up?"

"You bet! I'll be seeing you at five tomorrow morning."

The youngster ran off as quickly as he had appeared. As the back door slammed behind him, Nancy removed the bracelet and handed it to Hannah Gruen.

"Please put this away for me," she requested. "I shan't be gone long."

Nancy kissed her and promised to be careful. Seated in her convertible, her reddish-blonde hair blowing in the summer breeze as she drove along, Nancy made a charming picture. But her expression was serious and her thoughts were on the circus performer. The young detective wondered what kind of misfortune she had met.

Ten minutes later Nancy parked the car in the driveway of the riding academy and walked to Señor Roberto's office. Hitch, the stableman, greeted her in his usual glum manner. The groom, whom Nancy knew only by his nickname, never changed his dour expression.

"The boss ain't here," he muttered.

"When will Señor Roberto return?"

"How should I know?" the unpleasant man grumbled. He suddenly shook his finger at Nancy. "If you know what's good for you, Miss Drew, you'll stay away from circus ridin'."

"Circus riding?" Nancy asked, puzzled. "I haven't been doing any circus riding."

"Yes, you have, too." Hitch's voice was rising angrily. "That's what Roberto tries on everybody who shows a leanin' for it. But I'll tellin' you, quit it! Stop now! Right now!"

Nancy stared in amazement at Hitch, whose eyes were blazing. What could be behind his outburst, she wondered. A hatred of Roberto?

"Nobody what ain't been brought up in a circus has got any right to try imitatin' circus folks!" Hitch shouted. "I tell you—"

The tirade ended abruptly when the stableman saw Señor Roberto walking across the outdoor riding ring towards his office. The irate helper ambled off, saying he would bring her mare. Nancy stepped outside.

"Good afternoon, Miss Drew," the riding master said with a smile. "Sorry to be late."

"I didn't mind waiting," Nancy replied. "Hitch and I were talking. He—er—seemed a bit upset."

"About the circus, no doubt," Roberto commented. "Hitch will never get over his dismissal from Sims'. He doesn't talk about much else."

"I presume he's rather keyed up because the circus is coming here tomorrow," Nancy remarked.

"To tell you the truth, Miss Drew, Hitch is beside himself. He has declared he won't go near it, but I wonder if he can resist. Anyway, I'm going. I want to see what acts they have now and say hello to my old friends."

As Roberto finished speaking, Hitch led Nancy's mare into the ring. The beautiful grey horse nuzzled the girl as she stroked the animal's velvety nose and murmured:

"Belgian Star, you sweet old thing! We're going to have a good lesson today."

Nancy swung into the saddle and walked her horse counterclockwise several times around the ring. Then Señor Roberto called out:

"Trot!"

Automatically, Nancy sat still for few strides, then started to post. The riding master smiled in satisfaction at the rhythm and grace of Nancy's performance.

Next came the canter. Half an hour later, Nancy was ready for stunt riding. First, Hitch removed the saddle, looking darkly at Nancy as he carried it away.

Once more she mounted the horse, this time with only the blanket between her and the mare. Nancy slapped her gently on the flank and the horse began to canter slowly. Being an ex-circus horse, Belgian Star was considerate of her rider.

She seemed to know just the right speed to use, too, as Nancy stood up on the mare's back. Keeping her balance, Nancy went twice round the enclosure. On the third lap she caught a fleeting glimpse of a figure crouching on the ground outside the split-rail fence.

The next moment, a rock sailed through the air directly at Belgian Star's head. The horse reared almost straight up, and Nancy was thrown off!

· 2 ·

A Suspicious Groom

ON the far side of the ring Señor Roberto had witnessed the accident in alarm and dismay. He rushed towards Nancy, who lay still on the turf where she had fallen. As he reached her, the girl's eyelids flickered open.

"Miss Drew!" the riding master cried. "Are you all right?"

Nancy nodded slowly and struggled to a sitting position. Then, with Señor Roberto's assistance, she got to her feet. To the man's amazement, her first words were:

"Is Belgian Star all right?"

It was typical of Nancy not to think of herself first. She had been in many tight spots while solving the various mysteries that had come her way, but the safety of the innocent persons involved had always been her chief concern. Starting with *The Secret of Shadow Ranch*, she had proved herself adept in handling difficult situations and bringing many criminals to justice. This had been particularly true in her most recent case, which had come to be known as *The Secret in the Old Attic*.

"Miss Drew," said Señor Roberto, "you look very pale. We'll go into my office and I'll fix you some tea."

Nancy was not to be sidetracked in her concern for Belgian Star. The horse had left the ring and was now out of sight.

Nancy managed a wan smile. "I don't mean to seem ungrateful," she said, "but someone hurled a rock at Star's head. It may have injured her."

Señor Roberto looked worried. "I understand now why you were anxious about the mare," he said. "We'll look into this at once. Have you any idea who the person was?"

"No, I haven't," Nancy replied. "I didn't see his face."

Suddenly the riding master bellowed, "Hitch! Hitch! Come here at once!"

The stableman did not appear instantly. But after the third summons he ran from the building.

"Were you out here when Miss Drew fell?" the riding master asked him.

"Why, no, sir," the groom replied. "I didn't even know there'd been any trouble."

"Did you see anyone outside the fence?"

"No, sir."

"Did Belgian Star run into her stall?" Roberto questioned him.

"Yes, she did. Star seemed pretty excited. I've been tryin' to calm her down."

While the riding master explained to his stableman about the accident, Nancy noticed that Hitch was wearing the same kind of clothes and old soft hat as the figure she had seen on the ground. And his suit had fresh dirt on it! Nancy's suspicions were instantly aroused. She gazed beyond the fence to determine whether the man might have had time by now to make a circuitous route back to the stable.

"He could have done it easily," she told herself, staring at the thick woods which came up almost to the fence of the riding ring. "And Hitch is out of breath from running."

The man who had caused the accident could have crawled into the woods and returned to the academy without being seen.

Nancy turned to Hitch. "How did you get all that fresh dirt on the front of your clothes?"

Hitch suddenly looked uncomfortable.

"I guess I'd better tell the truth—seein' as how you'll probably find it out in the end," Hitch said. "I walked around through the woods to watch you do the circus stunts. While I was lookin', I seen a feller lyin' on the ground by the fence. The next thing I knew he threw somethin' at your horse. Then when I seen you fall off I got so scared I beat it. That's when I tripped and fell down in the dirt."

"Have you any idea who the man was?" Señor Roberto inquired in a cold voice.

Hitch said that he had not seen the man's face and was sorry now he had not waited to find out.

"I'm mighty glad you're all right, Miss Drew," Hitch added, and walked back to the stable.

There was nothing more Nancy could do. Despite the groom's story, she felt sure that he was the person who had thrown the stone. But why had he tried to harm her and Belgian Star?

"I'll certainly watch him from now on," Nancy decided.

She told Señor Roberto that she felt fully recovered from her spill, and if Belgian Star were all right, she wanted to continue her riding lesson.

Hitch brought Belgian Star from the stable. Nancy and the riding master carefully examined the mare's nose, and though there was a bruise on it, the horse did not seem to be suffering any pain.

"Are you game to go on with our lesson?" Nancy

asked the mare, putting her arms around the animal's gracefully arched neck.

In answer, Belgian Star went into the ring and waited for Nancy to climb on. This time she circled the ring several times before attempting to stand up on the horse's back.

"Am I imagining it or is someone peering at me from among those trees?" she asked herself, trying to shrug off a distrustful mood.

As she rounded the curve on the next lap, Nancy was sure she was not wrong—someone *was* watching her. A feeling of uneasiness came over her.

Nancy had just about decided to practise stunt riding when a voice hailed her. She turned abruptly to see two girls running from the woods. They climbed on to the fence, laughing.

"Bess! George!" Nancy cried. "Where did you come from?"

She immediately turned Belgian Star round and rode up to the fence. She noticed that Bess Marvin, blonde, blue-eyed, and several pounds heavier than Nancy, was holding a sketching pad and pencil in her hands.

Bess's cousin George Fayne leaned over the fence and patted Belgian Star. She was slim and athletic-looking. Her dark-brown hair was cut very short.

"Let's see you do some stunts," George urged.

"Yes, please do," said Bess. "I want to make several sketches."

Nancy agreed and then told the girls what had happened to her a short time ago and asked if they had seen a man running as they came through the woods. Neither of them had, but George offered to stand guard while Nancy did her trick riding.

Bess and George were amazed at their friend's proficiency as an equestrienne. Under Roberto's coaching Nancy somersaulted from Belgian Star and leaped back on the mare's back as the horse cantered round the ring.

"You're a whiz!" George said admiringly. "And you sure kept all this a secret."

"How did you find out about my taking these lessons?" Nancy asked as the girls walked towards the stable.

"From Hannah Gruen," George replied. "She's worried about you and this trick riding, Nancy."

"I know Hannah is concerned," the pretty sleuth answered. "But I've promised not to break any bones."

Nancy introduced her friends to Señor Roberto. Then she told them about the bracelet she had received from Aunt Eloise. Nancy asked the riding master if he had ever seen or heard about a horse-charm bracelet which had been presented to some circus performer by a queen.

"Why do you ask?" Señor Roberto wrinkled his brow, as if trying to remember something.

Nancy related the mysterious story connected with the bracelet. Señor Roberto said, upon reflection, that he had heard such a tale but could not recall who had told it.

"I seem to recollect, though," he added slowly, "that the story involved a strange disappearance. Whether it was the bracelet or the owner or the giver I don't know."

He called to Hitch and asked him whether he had ever heard about a horse-charm bracelet. The riding master briefly recounted what Nancy had told him. The stableman looked first at Nancy and then at his employer. Finally, in a gruff tone, he replied:

"Yes, I heard about a bracelet like that pony one when I was workin' for Sims' Circus."

"Do you remember who told you?" Nancy asked.

The groom thought for several seconds, then said he could not recall. Shrugging, he added, "You know how it is in the circus. All kinds o' stories get around."

Although Nancy was disappointed not to learn more, she was hopeful of being able to question various members of Sims' Circus the next day. By the following evening she might have the answer to the riddle of the bracelet!

For this reason getting up at four thirty the next morning did not seem like such a chore. Teddy was sitting on the doorstep when Nancy arrived at the Browns' house. The two set off for the circus grounds in Nancy's convertible.

It seemed as if all the children in River Heights had gathered to watch the big tents being put up. They were running in every direction so as not to miss anything. The good-natured workmen did not seem to mind the excitement and confusion.

Nancy had a hard time keeping track of Teddy. For a while she held on to his hand, running along with him as he darted from place to place.

A short respite came as he paused to watch the elephants being watered in a large tent. It was a thrill for the small boy when a man handed him a bucket and and asked if he would like to let Old Jumbo, the biggest elephant, drink out of it.

"Can I really!" Teddy cried gleefully.

Just then a girl's voice called, "Hi, Nancy!"

It was George. She had her little nephew in tow. The two girls chatted for a few seconds, then Nancy turned back to watch Teddy. He was not in sight!

She looked round the tent. Not seeing Teddy there Nancy dashed outside. Her eyes roamed over the crowd. Finally she spotted the red-haired youngster and hurried towards him.

But before Nancy could reach him, she was horrified to see a large pole on a truck next to the boy begin to slide. If he did not get out of the way, it would strike him!

"Teddy!" Nancy screamed. "Run!"

· 3 ·

The Cruel Ringmaster

FOR a harrowing second Teddy Brown did not seem to understand what Nancy was saying. The heavy pole, sliding down from the top of the pile, was going to fall on him at any second!

"Teddy!" Nancy screamed again. "Run! Run!"

This time the little boy obeyed. He jumped out of the path of the pole in the nick of time. It landed on the ground with a tremendous thud and began to roll. But Teddy Brown, running to Nancy, was safe.

She dashed up and threw her arms about the youngster. Her heart was pounding wildly.

"Oh, Teddy, you gave me such a fright," she said, trembling.

"I'm sorry, Nancy," the little boy replied. "I won't leave you again."

Teddy kept his word. During the rest of their tour of the circus grounds, he kept tight hold of Nancy's hand.

There was so much to see—the wild animals, the beautiful horses, and the astonishingly large cafeteria where the circus people ate.

"Can we have breakfast here, Nancy?" the little boy asked.

"I'm afraid not, Teddy," the girl replied. "They don't sell food here. The cafeteria is only for the circus people."

"Can't we buy something to eat?" Teddy persisted. "Popcorn or hot dogs? They always sell those at circuses."

Nancy smiled and explained that the refreshment stands were not open yet. Teddy was so hungry by this time that it was hard to dissuade him from going into the cafeteria tent. As he stood hungrily eyeing the long row of portable stoves on which the circus chefs were cooking, a man brushed by them rudely, pushing the little boy out of his way.

The man was tall and had a rather long moustache. His black hair stood straight up and his eyes flashed. On one arm was a large blue-and-red tattoo mark.

"Is he one of the freaks?" Teddy asked loud enough for the man to hear. The little boy had never seen a tattoo.

The man stopped short, turned, and glared at the youngster. Then, pointing a menacing finger at him, he exclaimed:

"Get out of here!"

Teddy leaned against Nancy, who tried to excuse the boy, but the man would not listen.

"I said, get out of here! Visitors aren't supposed to be

in the cafeteria. Strangers are a nuisance, anyhow. If I had my way, there wouldn't be one inside these grounds until performance time."

Nancy led Teddy away. He was clinging to her and shaking like a leaf. She patted his shoulder and told him that he must not be frightened. As a pleasant-looking woman, carrying costumes over her arm, passed them, Nancy stopped her and asked about the man with the moustache.

"That's our ringmaster. His name is Kroon—Reinhold Kroon."

"You mean he's the one who snaps the whip and makes the horses go?" Teddy asked, his eyes wide with interest. He had already forgotten that the man had been unkind to him.

"Oh, he does more than that," the woman replied, smiling. "He announces all the acts. He used to be a horseman, but now he's practically in charge of this whole circus."

"Why doesn't he like people?" Teddy asked her.

"I don't know very much about him," the woman answered. "I help with the sewing. Mr Kroon doesn't seem to be happy, though."

After a few minutes of further conversation, Nancy asked the woman if she had been with the circus long.

"Several years."

Nancy then inquired if the seamstress had ever known anyone who owned a horse-charm bracelet.

"No, I haven't," she replied. "Why? Does it have something to do with this circus?"

"It might," Nancy replied. "Where can I find Mr Sims?"

The seamstress said that Mr Sims was rarely at the circus. In fact, he had not travelled with them for several weeks. Mr Kroon was apparently in charge now. She suggested that Nancy ask him about the bracelet.

"Oh, please don't go back to him," Teddy begged.

Since Nancy did not wish to upset the boy, she decided to question the ringmaster later. She thanked the seamstress for her information, then she and Teddy walked away.

"We'd better go home now," Nancy told him. "I'm ready for breakfast myself. Suppose I pick you up at nine o'clock and we'll go watch the parade together."

"That'll be swell," Teddy agreed eagerly.

When Nancy reached home, she found Hannah Gruen preparing breakfast and asked whether her father had returned. The housekeeper shook her head.

"Your father did telephone, though," Hannah reported. "He was disappointed that you weren't here."

"Did he have anything special to tell me?" Nancy asked.

"No, except to say that he would have to be away for a while—he didn't know just how long."

Nancy looked wistful. She missed her father very much when his legal work took him out of town. She enjoyed discussing his cases with him and also getting his advice on any mysteries which she happened to be working on at the moment.

"Well, I guess we're ready to sit down," said Mrs Gruen. "Did you find out anything about your bracelet at the circus, Nancy?'

"No, I didn't. But I'll talk to more of the people later. The circus will be here for two or three days, I believe."

At nine o'clock Nancy and Teddy were on their way to the main street of River Heights along which the circus parade would come. Although the parade was not due to arrive for another half-hour, the street already was lined with hundreds of people. Nancy and Teddy had to walk four blocks from the centre of town before they could find a place on the kerb.

A few minutes later they heard a band. The music grew louder and louder, and presently they could see the marching players. Teddy clapped his hands and jumped up and down gleefully.

"Here come the elephants," Nancy announced, and Teddy craned his neck to see the enormous animals swinging up the street.

Men and women attired in gay costumes accompanied the elephants. The men were seated astride the animals' backs, but the girls were walking alongside them. Occasionally they would seat themselves on the elephants' curled-up trunks and ride for half a block before jumping off.

"Gee, I bet that would be fun," said Teddy. "Oh, here comes Cinderella in a gold carriage."

"She's the main attraction in the circus, I understand," Nancy remarked. "Her name is Lolita. She does a very daring aerial act."

As the carriage glided by, drawn by four beautiful white horses, Lilita waved to the people, who clapped their hands and shouted. But the lovely, dark-haired circus star did not smile in return.

"Why is she so sad?" Teddy asked. "She looks like Cinderella did after her carriage turned into a pumpkin."

"I wonder myself," Nancy said.

A moment after the girl had passed, the parade suddenly halted. Without warning Teddy left Nancy. He dashed into the street and ran down to Cinderella's carriage. Reaching up, he opened the door and hopped inside.

Nancy was at the boy's heels. No sooner had Teddy seated himself beside Lolita, than Nancy opened the door and requested him to come out.

For the first time Lolita smiled. She put her arm around Teddy and said, "Let him stay. He's the only one who has ever done this. I think it's rather nice."

Nancy closed the door. Smiling, she said, "As soon as you want Teddy to leave, don't hesitate to say so. I'll walk along beside the carriage and take care of him when he gets out."

Teddy, meanwhile, looked wistfully at Cinderella. "Why do you look so sad?" he asked.

"Do I really?" the girl countered, then added, "You've heard how unhappy the real Cinderella was because she lost her prince, haven't you? Well, I guess I'm sad for the same reason."

Lolita said no more. And Teddy, not understanding the implication in her words, turned to watch the people on the sidewalk.

Everything went smoothly for about two blocks, then Nancy heard the sudden, sharp clop of horses' hoofs behind her. Looking over her shoulder, she saw the ringmaster galloping towards her. Quickly she jumped to the sidewalk to avoid being run down.

To her dismay, Kroon stopped at Cinderella's carriage. Reaching inside, he grabbed Teddy up in his arms and planted him firmly in front of him on the horse.

"You crazy kid!" he shouted. "What are you trying to do? Ruin my circus?"

Unceremoniously he lifted Teddy out of the saddle and plunked him down on the kerb. Nancy started to tell the irate ringmaster that his actions were quite unwarranted, since Lolita had said the child might ride with her, but Kroon rode off in a hurry. There were so many animals and circus people to look at—riders, clowns, giants, and midgets—that both Nancy and Teddy soon forgot the unpleasant incident.

Both were eager to attend the afternoon performance and arrived early at the circus grounds. Nancy wore an attractive blue dress and had slipped the horse-charm bracelet over her wrist. Bess and George, who had her young nephew with her, joined Nancy and Teddy. They had front-row seats in one of the centre boxes.

The performance began with a second parade for the benefit of those who had not seen the one on the street. When it was over, the entrance gate opened and seven clowns came running in. Teddy shrieked in delight.

One clown, dressed as a tattered hobo, had a little fox terrier with him which did tricks. Another clown, who was dressed as a farmer, was wearing a beard that reached to his knees. With it, he tickled the ears of a comical-looking cow, composed of two clowns. The fifth clown represented a barrel and did all sorts of tricks rolling around quite like one.

The last two were dressed in Pierrot clown suits. One carried a tall ladder. Just before he reached the spot where Nancy and her friends were seated, he planted the ladder upright in the ground and held on to it. The other clown, named Pietro, began to climb up. When he reached the top, the clown below suddenly let go and walked off.

"Oh!" everyone under the tent cried.

To their amazement, the clown on the ladder did not fall. He balanced himself skilfully, swaying back and forth above the ring. As everyone realized that this was a trick of great cleverness, and not just a clownish act, they clapped loudly.

"It's going to be even harder for him to climb down," George observed tensely.

The audience watched breathlessly as the clown slowly lowered himself without falling. He turned in a complete circle to acknowledge the loud applause.

As he bowed low before Nancy's group, a startled look came over his face. The clown walked forward and stared at Nancy's bracelet.

"Where did you get this, miss?" Pietro asked in a low voice.

Before the startled girl could reply, a whistle sounded and the band began to play. The clown hurriedly said, "I must speak to you after the show. Please meet me beside King Kat's cage."

· 4 ·

An Amazing Aerialist

"PIETRO!" Nancy called as the clown moved off. "Please tell me—"

But the performer did not turn round. It was not until he had completed a full circuit of the ring doing his amusing antics that he stopped to speak to her again.

"Where did you get the bracelet?" Pietro whispered as he completed a triple somersault.

Teddy Brown clapped so loudly he nearly drowned Nancy's answer. "A New York shop. But it came from Europe."

"Do you know where the missing horse charm is?" the clown asked.

"No."

"I do."

"Who has it?" Nancy questioned eagerly.

Pietro had no opportunity to answer, for at that moment a whistle summoned all the clowns from the ring. Several acts followed. Nancy found them intriguing but could not keep her mind entirely on the circus. Her thoughts reverted constantly to the clown's words and his request that she meet him at the end of the show. Certainly there *was* some secret about her charm bracelet that was not pure legend!

Presently it was time for the main act. All the lights were dimmed, except the spotlights on the centre ring. Kroon, dressed in striped trousers, Prince Albert coat, and wearing a high silk hat, walked to the microphone.

"Ladies and gentlemen," he announced, "you are about to witness the world's most daring, most stupendous aerial act! Lolita, our Cinderella, will meet her prince in mid-air and dance for him. But at the stroke of twelve, this brief romance will end. Ladies and gentlemen, do not take your eyes off this colossal spectacle!"

As the ringmaster retired, the spotlights picked up a small Cinderella carriage being drawn round the ring by two white wooden steeds. In it sat beautiful, fairy-like Lolita, dressed in a white, silver-spangled robe.

The applause was thunderous as attendants attached the carriage to pulleys and Cinderella was slowly pulled up a slanting wire to the top of the tent. Daintily Lolita stood up, discarded her robe, and stepped out in white satin acrobatic tights to a tiny platform which was suspended from the ceiling.

At once, additional floodlights showed four young men aerialists, signalling for her attention. Smiling, Lolita waited as each one swung towards her, executing a simple dance act on the trapezes to tango, rhumba, and polka tunes. But as each man knelt on the platform and indicated that he wanted to marry Cinderella, Lolita shook her head and he swung away.

As she stood there, acting discouraged, suddenly a handsome prince in a gleaming silver costume appeared in the spotlight beside her. The two smiled, then kissed.

"Prince Charming!" announced Bess, gazing enthralled at the performance. But her friends scarcely heard her. Their eyes were fixed on the acrobatic drama far above them. To the strains of a waltz, Cinderella would dance a few steps alone on a trapeze, then swing towards her prince. After executing some steps together on the aerial swing, she would leave him and repeat the solo, each time in more difficult rhythms. At the end of the third solo, Lolita promised to marry him.

After an embrace, the girl suddenly became aware of a striking gong. One, two— The prince held her close. Three, four— The girl tried to pull away. The gong kept striking! Eleven—twelve!"

Cinderella swung towards the platform where the carriage had been. But alas, the sides of the gorgeous carriage and the white horses had tumbled off and dropped into a net below. Now, instead, merely a pumpkin, drawn by mice, remained. The aerialist in a barely perceptible motion had slipped out of her white satin spangled tights and now stood in a ragged black costume.

"Oh!" shrieked Teddy, to whom all this was very real. "Poor Cinderella! Nancy, when will the prince—" The little boy stopped abruptly.

Lolita, about to climb into the pumpkin, suddenly swayed, then seemed to lose her footing. She plunged downward towards the net.

There was a momentary hush as the audience wondered if this was part of the act. But the silence was followed by cries of alarm when Lolita lay still.

"Oh," murmured Teddy. "Is she—"

"Lolita must have fainted," Nancy told him, and in her heart she hoped it was nothing more serious than this.

From the shadowy stage entrances rushed many willing hands to help the stricken aerialist, among them Pietro. Ringmaster Kroon waved them all aside. Walking under the net, he hissed at Lolita, loud enough for Nancy to hear:

"Get up! You're making fools of all of us! The show will be ruined! Climb out of there and take a bow!"

Nancy leaned across to Bess, who seemed frozen with fear, and picked up a pair of field glasses which lay on her friend's lap. Through them she could see Lolita, her face chalk-white, slowly open her eyes. Pietro reached up and tenderly patted her cheek.

"Leave her alone!" Kroon thundered at the clown. "And get out of here!"

Pietro glared at his employer. It was evident that his fondness for the girl overshadowed obedience to the ringmaster. He stood still, speaking in low tones to Lolita. Finally, Kroon yanked the clown up by his big ruffled collar and sent him sprawling to the ground. Turning back to Lolita, the harsh manager cried:

"Stand up!"

This time the girl obeyed, rising slowly and stepping to the edge of the net, where she was helped down by attendants. Lolita took bow after bow amid tumultuous applause, but Nancy felt that the girl was using all of her willpower to remain on her feet.

As Lolita left the tent, Kroon hurried into the ring. "And so," he said, "Cinderella lost her prince. But only temporarily! If you want to see how he found her by matching the glass slipper she wore, come to this evening's performance. Reserve your seats on the way out! And now, our next act—"

George whispered to her, "Nancy, do you think this was just a come-on, or couldn't Lolita finish the act?"

"I'm afraid she's ill, George. I'll find out when I meet Pietro."

The last act was a clever bareback riding performance with a triumphant final pageant which included the clowns. As soon as it was over, Nancy asked George to take Teddy home, then started for King Kat's cage to meet the circus clown.

Pietro was waiting and beckoned her to follow him a short distance away from the cage. The clown seemed very ill at ease, almost frightened, as he said:

"I'll talk fast. Visitors aren't allowed here. If Kroon should find me talking to you, he might discharge me, and that mustn't happen."

"Can't we go some place where he won't see us?" Nancy asked. She did not want to miss the opportunity to hear everything the clown might want to tell her.

"No, no!" he said quickly. "This is the story. Lolita wears a horse charm on a necklace. It matches the charms on your bracelet and I noticed one is missing. Lolita once said she thought hers came from another piece of jewellery."

"Oh, I must see the necklace!" Nancy said. "Please take me to Lolita."

The clown shook his head. He said that the aerialist was resting and must not be disturbed before the evening performance.

"It's Kroon we must be careful about." Pietro sighed. "I just don't want him to become angry at Lolita."

"I understand," Nancy agreed. "Go ahead with your story."

Pietro said that Lolita was Mr and Mrs Kroon's adopted daughter. She had lived with them since she was eight years old.

"Have the Kroons and Lolita always been in the circus?" Nancy asked.

The clown nodded and said that Lolita's own parents had been trapeze artists.

"They were known as the Flying Flanders," he explained. "I'm told they were very fine performers."

"What were their names?" Nancy questioned.

"John and Lola Flanders. I never knew them," the clown went on. "The story was that when Lolita was eight years old, her parents were killed in Europe while performing their flying act. It was then that the Kroons brought Lolita to the United States."

"And you think Lolita's horse charm might have belonged on my bracelet?" Nancy asked.

"It's possible. I just thought you two might get together and find out."

"I'll certainly do that," Nancy promised.

She asked Pietro if Lolita's parents had taught their daughter to be an aerialist.

"Oh, yes," he replied. "But after their death she was trained by other artists as well."

The clown smiled slightly, then said that he considered Lolita the finest aerialist in the world.

"But her foster father makes her work too hard," he said angrily. "Kroon doesn't care about anything but money."

"He does seem rather dictatorial," Nancy remarked.

The clown looked at her. "That's putting it mildly. Kroon is cruel, and besides, I don't trust him."

Nancy wondered why Pietro distrusted the ringmaster, but the young man did not explain further. He changed the subject and said:

"About the horse charm. The one Lolita wears was given to her by her mother when she was only five years old. That was thirteen years ago. I suppose it's only coincidence that the charm looks like those on your bracelet," he said.

"I'm not so sure of that," Nancy rejoined.

Quickly she related what she knew of the charm bracelet's history; that the shopkeeper, from whom her Aunt Eloise had purchased the jewellery, had hinted at a mystery. The original owner, supposedly a circus performer, had sold the bracelet because she was in trouble.

Pietro stared at Nancy in amazement. "That might well be," he said. "I have suspected for a long time that there's some secret in connection with the Kroons and Lolita. Whenever I suggest this to her, she becomes frightened and asks me not to talk about it."

Suddenly a look of alarm came over the clown's face. "Here comes Kroon now. Run!" he advised. Like a shot he was off, dodging among the various animal cages and trucks until he was out of sight.

Nancy decided not to avoid the ringmaster. She wanted to speak to him and find out about Lolita's condition. But she had no opportunity. Kroon, instead of passing her, turned abruptly into a near-by tent.

When she looked inside, he already had disappeared.

Nancy wondered whether or not to question any other circus people about Lolita's real parents. She concluded that it would be better to talk with the girl first. Nancy decided to attend the evening performance. Perhaps after it she would have a chance to interview the aerialist.

"I have a date with Ned," she reminded herself. "I'm sure he'll be glad to come to the circus."

At seven o'clock Ned Nickerson, Emerson College's star football player, arrived at the Drew home. Nancy showed him her gold horse bracelet and told him of the new mystery, then she asked him if he would take her to the circus.

"Glad to." He grinned. "But listen here, young lady," Ned said, "don't get yourself so mixed up with clowns and aerialists that you can't even find time to talk to me!"

Nancy chuckled, but she knew Ned had good reason to scold her. Many times when they had a date she changed the plans completely and involved him in some mystery she was trying to solve.

"Lolita is the most wonderful aerialist I have ever seen," Nancy remarked as they neared the circus grounds.

"Two in the front row as near the centre as possible," Ned told the ticket seller.

"Sorry, sir," the man replied, "there's not even standing room left."

Nancy's heart sank. She stepped up to the window. "It's very important that I see the show this evening. Couldn't we just—?"

"Sorry, miss," the man said firmly. "Not one more person can be admitted."

• 5 •

A Strange Attack

NANCY looked pleadingly at the ticket seller. Something about her expression made him ask:

"Why is it so necessary that you see the performance? Some friend of yours in it?"

"In a way, yes," Nancy replied. She did not want to tell him about the mystery, but she did want to get inside the grounds. Suddenly Nancy had an idea and said, "Couldn't we go in just to see the animals and the side shows?"

The ticket seller thought a moment. "I'd like to let you into the performance under the big top, but it's against the fire rules to exceed the seating capacity."

"We understand," said Nancy, "but you haven't answered my questions. There's nothing in the fire rules that forbids people from walking around to look at the animals and the side shows, is there?"

The man had to admit there was not. He called to the guard who was taking tickets at the gate and told him to let in the young lady and her escort.

Nancy and Ned thanked him and hurried inside. Ned inquired what the next move was to be.

"Pretty soon all the animals and the freaks will be going in the parade," he reminded her. "Then what?"

Nancy smiled. She told him that her plan was to accomplish almost everything that she wanted to do before the performance began.

"First of all, I want to locate Lolita and have a talk with her."

She walked up to one of the midgets who had just finished entertaining the crowd with a card trick. "Will you please tell me where Lolita's tent is?" she asked him.

He replied in a squeaky, thin voice, "I ain't allowed to tell."

Nancy was taken aback. She wondered whether the little man was just trying to be funny or whether this really was a rule of the circus. Nancy moved on to the fat lady who was seated on a platform next to the midget and repeated her question.

"Sorry, miss," the twenty-five stone woman answered, "but we're not allowed to give out any information. Mr Kroon's rule."

Nancy decided that she would have to find Lolita's tent by herself!

She left Ned watching the fire-eater and hurried off. Up one aisle of tents and down another she went. But there was nothing to indicate that Lolita occupied one the tents.

Walking to the outer fringe of the tent colony, Nancy saw several trailers. Perhaps Lolita lived in one of these!

"I'll just wander around among them and see what I can find out," Nancy decided.

Luck was with her. As she approached the first trailer, Nancy could hear two persons arguing heatedly.

"But, Father, I don't feel well enough to perform." It was the young aerialist speaking!

"You'll perform tonight and put on a good act, too!" the harsh voice of the ringmaster came to Nancy's ears.

"But I'm so afraid I'll fall again," Lolita said.

For the next two minutes, Kroon gave the aerialist a

severe tongue-lashing. Nancy decided that the man was completely without reason. She was so incensed at him and so sorry for Lolita that she wanted to rush in at once and help the poor girl.

Suddenly the man thundered, "I'll give you exactly fifteen minutes to make up your mind, Lolita! Then I'll be back. You'd better decide to perform. If you don't, you'll be sorry. I'll discharge every single friend of yours in this circus!"

With that, he rushed out of the trailer and strode off. His face was livid and Nancy again wondered whether the man could be in his right mind.

When he was out of sight, she went to the door of the trailer. About to knock, she heard crying within. Nancy hesitated for several moments, wondering whether she should disturb the unhappy aerialist or not.

Her sympathy and desire to help got the better of Nancy. She tapped on the door. At first there was no response, then a tearful voice said:

"Come in."

Lolita was startled at seeing Nancy in the doorway and did not look pleased about it. Almost at once, though, she smiled, because Nancy's warm expression revealed that she wanted to be friendly. Without mentioning the fact that she knew Lolita had been crying or that she had overheard Kroon's threat, Nancy held up the beautiful charm bracelet.

"Pietro told me you have a gold charm that matches these little horses," she said. "I just couldn't resist the temptation to come and see if by chance it might be the one which is missing from this bracelet."

Lolita misunderstood. Frowning, she said, "Oh, my goodness! You don't think I stole it?"

Nancy was aghast. "No, no," she said quickly. "I'm

sorry. I'm just interested in knowing if you've ever seen my bracelet or heard anything about its history."

Lolita shook her head, but she fingered the exquisite little horses. Then, going to a bureau drawer, she brought out a dainty gold chain. Attached was a golden horse. The miniature animal, wrought exactly like those on Nancy's bracelet, was a duplicate of the cantering horse.

"Your bracelet may may have belonged to my lovely mother," said Lolita sadly. "She died when I was only eight years old, but I remember very well how she looked."

"Perhaps she sold the bracelet," Nancy suggested.

Lolita agreed this was possible, but it would be difficult to determine the fact definitely. Whenever she asked Mr or Mrs Kroon about her parents, the couple changed the subject. The reason they gave was that they did not like to talk about the Flanders' terrible accident. Leaning close to Nancy, she whispered:

"Sometimes I wonder if it's true that my parents are dead."

"Would you like me to help you find out?" Nancy asked on the spur of the moment.

"Oh, could you?" Lolita exclaimed, giving Nancy an impetuous hug.

Nancy told the girl that she had solved a few mysteries and would be glad to find out what she could. She asked if Lolita could give her any clues at all, but the young aerialist shook her head.

"As I told you before, my foster parents are very close-mouthed. Sometimes I think there must be a reason why they won't tell me anything."

Suddenly Lolita looked at a clock on the wall. The fifteen minutes were up!

"You'd better go now," she said abruptly. "Mr Kroon will be here any moment and he mustn't see you." Suddenly Lolita again put her arms around Nancy. "I never saw you until a few minutes ago," she said, "but already you are my friend. I feel much better than I did before you came. Doing my high-wire act seemed impossible then, but now I'll be able to put on a good show."

As they stepped outside, Lolita asked where Nancy would be sitting and said she would wave to her. Learning that the girl and her escort had been unable to obtain tickets, Lolita declared that she would get two for her. The aerialist called to a man who was walking past the trailer.

"Oh, Dan," she said. "Come here quickly, please."

As the man hurried over, Lolita introduced him to Nancy as Dan Webster, one of the horse trainers. Suddenly Lolita laughed, then remarked that she had failed to ask her caller's name. When Nancy told her, Lolita said to Dan Webster:

"Please get Nancy two tickets for the special seats and hurry. Bring them back here."

As Dan hurried off, Nancy saw Kroon approaching. Quickly she ducked around the corner out of sight.

Reaching the trailer, Kroon glared at Lolita. "Well, what's your answer?" he stormed.

"I feel better, Father. I'll do my act," Lolita said quietly.

The man gave a raucous laugh, took her by the hand, and led her away. "Get into your costume," he ordered.

As Nancy waited for Dan Webster to return with the tickets, her dislike for Kroon mounted. She decided to make every effort to find out for Lolita more about her real parents. The fact that the aerialist herself had doubts of their death was a further incentive to the young sleuth.

The horse trainer returned in a few minutes and walked with Nancy as far as the side shows. On the way she told him of her endeavours to learn trick riding from Señor Roberto who used to be with Sims' Circus.

"So this is where Roberto has been hiding!" Dan Webster exclaimed. "Everybody wondered where he'd gone. I'll certainly have to run out to see him tomorrow morning. Where is his riding academy?"

Nancy gave him directions and then left the trainer. She found Ned and they hurried into the tent.

The seats were in the front row of a box right at the ringside. As the performance was about to start, Nancy noticed that the other seats in the box were empty. With the house sold out, why had no one claimed them, she wondered.

When the parade ended, Nancy watched eagerly for the clowns to appear. Every one of them came out except Pietro.

"I wonder what happened to him?" she asked herself.

Nancy was so worried that she hardly saw the funny antics going on near her. Finally she leaned out and asked one of the clowns where Pietro was.

"I haven't seen him," the clown replied, and went on with his stunts.

The act ended and still Pietro did not appear.

"Maybe Kroon is responsible," Nancy thought.

What if the ringmaster had begun to carry out his threat of dismissing all of Lolita's friends!

A few moments later Kroon stepped to the centre of the ring and announced that the next performance would be a horse act.

"This is the world's smartest horse!" the ringmaster proclaimed. "He thinks like a human being."

All the lights went out except the spotlight on the ring. A beautiful pure-white horse trotted in from the wings.

Nancy was vaguely aware that a man had slid into the seat directly behind her. But she was too intrigued by what was going on in the ring to pay particular attention to the latecomer.

Suddenly she felt something tight against her throat. The next moment, Nancy realized that she was being choked!

· 6 ·

A Threat

As the choking sensation increased, Nancy's hand flew to her throat. To the girl's horror she felt a cord around her neck. It was being drawn tighter and tighter.

She tugged at it frantically but could not remove or even loosen the cord. Objects in the circus were swimming before Nancy's eyes and her breath was coming in gasps.

Ned turned just as she was about to black out. Nancy reached out towards him, then fainted. Aghast, he caught her and quickly unwound the cord.

She gave a tremendous gasp and a slight tremor ran through her body. Ned massaged her neck and arms.

In a few moments her breathing became normal again.

Nancy sat up and looked around her. Then, suddenly recalling the awful ordeal of a moment ago, she clutched her throat. When she found no cord constricting it, she looked questioningly at Ned. Had she imagined the whole thing?

"Are you all right?" Ned asked anxiously.

"Y-yes. What happened to me?"

He told her, pointing to a souvenir whip on the floor. Then he added, "I'll find out who did this devilish thing! It must have been the work of a maniac! I'll go and inform the police."

Nancy now recalled having heard someone sit down in the seat behind her. He must be the guilty person! But turning around, Nancy saw that the seat was now vacant. Idly she picked up the short whip which had been used to strangle her. It was the type sold as souvenirs at the circus.

Seeing one of the vendors, Nancy summoned him. Suspended around his neck was a large basket in which he carried cold drinks, boxes of popcorn, bags of peanuts, and a variety of souvenirs, including the toy whips.

"Did you make a sale to a man who was sitting behind me?" Nancy questioned the vendor.

"Naw," he replied. "Whaddaya want to buy?"

Nancy put a hand in her pocket and pulled out a fifty-cent piece, saying she would take a bag of peanuts. As the vendor gave her the change, she asked him whether he had sold one of the whips to anyone nearby.

"I ain't sold one of these here ringmaster's whips all evening," the vendor said disgustedly. "I dunno what's the matter with everybody. Business is mighty slow." He moved off.

"Ringmaster's whip," Nancy repeated, her mind flying to Kroon.

As she thought about the recent episode, the young sleuth decided that the person who had tried to choke her must have brought the whip with him—perhaps in his pocket. When Ned returned, she whispered to him:

"I'm inclined to think the choker might have been somebody connected with the circus."

Ned agreed and said that the box might be reserved for circus personnel. He remarked that this would narrow their search for her assailant, although the policeman to whom he had reported the incident felt little could be done without a better clue than the whip.

"But let's wait until after Lolita's act before we investigate," Nancy said. "She especially wanted me to be here this evening."

As soon as the act started, Ned was glad that they had waited. Not only was the Cinderella performance artistic, but intricate and difficult as well. One misstep on the part of Lolita or any of her princes could possibly mean their death or at least a nasty fall!

Nancy hardly dared breathe during the show, hoping that Lolita really did feel better and that she would not faint again. Did the aerialist know that Pietro had not performed? Would this make a difference to her? Nancy felt sure that there was a strong attachment between the two.

"Oh!" the crowd suddenly gasped.

Lolita had almost missed grabbing the hands of one of the princes in a swing from trapeze to trapeze. But she made it and her audience settled back, their hearts beating excitedly.

From the point where Lolita had fainted during the afternoon performance, the story was now carried to its completion, as Ringmaster Kroon had announced.

The handsome prince whom Cinderella had promised to marry while at the ball swung gracefully to her platform. In his hand was a glass slipper. There was a short ceremony at the top of the tent. When he found that it fitted Lolita's foot, he embraced her. Then came a most fascinating trapeze act, with the two swinging back and forth, first alone, then together. The pair kept in perfect time with the lilting background music. The audience went wild in its applause.

The happy couple on the thirty-foot-high trapeze swung themselves to the platform. As the clapping continued, Lolita suddenly looked in Nancy's direction. Sweetly and daintily, she blew a kiss to her new friend. Nancy smiled and waved in return.

The sides of the gleaming coach and the two white steeds and Cinderella's spangled dress were drawn up by pulleys. Lolita put on the beautiful white ball gown as the pumpkin and mice were covered by the stately carriage and horses. Then she and her prince stepped inside and were brought down to the ground. They stepped out, took bow after bow amid the thunderous applause, then hurried away.

"That was superb," Ned remarked. "Anything else would seem tame. I'd just as soon go. How about you, Nancy?"

Nancy confessed that she was ready to leave, since she wanted to do some sleuthing. They hurried to the exit.

"Where do you suggest we start looking for that strangler?" Ned asked her.

"Suppose we find out about the box. The man must have had a ticket to it."

The ticket booth was closed, but Nancy saw the

attendant and asked him who owned Box AA.

"The house," he said. "It's always kept for special people, like the mayor. I understand some well-known couple used it tonight. The rest of the seats in the box were vacant."

Nancy suppressed a smile at the words "some well-known couple," and thanked the ticket seller for the information. She and Ned walked on.

"I'm more convinced than ever," she said, "that my attacker was someone who works here."

"But why?" Ned asked. "You haven't any enemies in the circus. Or have you?"

"I must have, but I'm sure I don't know why, Ned."

"Then you'd better leave this place and never come back."

"And leave the mystery unsolved?" Nancy objected.

As Ned shrugged resignedly, Nancy said she would like to find out why Pietro had not taken part in the evening performance. She wondered if it might have something to do with the mystery surrounding Lolita.

Nancy learned from one of the other clowns that Pietro had been taken suddenly ill. His friend thought it was nothing serious, and that Pietro would be able to perform the next day.

"Would you mind giving him a note?" Nancy asked, thinking there might be another reason for his skipping the performance and she could talk to him more freely at home about the mystery.

"Glad to," the clown replied.

Taking paper and pencil from her bag, Nancy quickly scribbled a message. She asked Pietro to come to her house before nine o'clock the next morning, as she was leaving at nine-thirty for a riding lesson. If he could not come then, she suggested that he make it between shows and bring Lolita if possible.

Ned now insisted that the rest of the evening be spent doing something that had no relation to the mystery. Nancy laughingly agreed, and they joined a group of friends at Bess Marvin's home.

It was late when Nancy reached her own house and said goodnight to Ned. As soon as she was in her room, Nancy's mind reverted to her harrowing experience with the whip.

"What could have been the reason for it?" she wondered, pulling her dress over her head. A wild thought struck Nancy. Had Kroon found out she was interested in helping Lolita, and therefore was afraid of some mysterious affairs of his own being uncovered? If so, he might very well have wanted to put a stop to her sleuthing.

As Nancy looked down at the floor, she noticed a small folded sheet of paper. It must have dropped from her dress, she thought. Puzzled, she picked it up and opened the sheet. Nancy stared at the ominous, crudely printed message.

Stay away from the circus and everybody in it!

· 7 ·

Stunt Riding

DUMBFOUNDED, Nancy reread the warning. It occurred to her that as the would-be strangler had pulled the whip around her neck he probably had slid the note into a pocket of her dress.

"Of course I shan't pay any attention," she resolved. "But I'd better be on my guard. Now I'm sure someone in the circus is my enemy."

Nancy examined the note carefully, but as far as she could see, there was nothing to indicate who had written it. She laid it in a desk drawer.

The next morning Nancy was up early and immediately put on her riding habit. She finished breakfast and tidied her room before nine o'clock, hoping that Pietro might show up. Nancy waited until the last moment before leaving for the riding academy, but the circus clown did not put in an appearance.

Nancy enjoyed her lesson with Señor Roberto, who smiled encouragingly at her performance. When he was summoned to the telephone, she rode round the outdoor ring several times, practising what she had learned that morning—somersaulting from the mare.

As Nancy halted Belgian Star, she noticed that Dan

Webster, the horse trainer from Sims' Circus, was standing in the doorway of the academy. He nodded his head in greeting and called out:

"Very fine riding, Miss Drew."

Nancy somersaulted from Belgian Star's back and stood smiling at the man from the circus.

"Say," he said admiringly, "if anything should go wrong in one of our bareback acts, I'll call on you to replace the rider. How about it?"

Nancy was sure that Dan Webster was teasing her, and she laughed gaily, making no reply. But the horse trainer did not smile.

"I'm serious," he stated. "You do these trick bareback stunts as well as many riders in the circus. I meant it when I said that should we have an unexpected opening I'd like to call on you."

Before Nancy had a chance to reply, Señor Roberto returned from his office. Seeing his old friend Dan Webster, he threw his arms about the man and kissed him on each cheek. In his excitement he spoke partly in English and partly in Spanish.

"*Si, si*, it is so good to see you, *amigo mio*. And you look so fine. How is everything at Sims?"

Dan Webster's face clouded. "Not so good, Roberto. Since you left, things have been getting worse. I think the people in the troupe are discouraged."

"You mean because of Kroon?" Roberto asked.

The riding master explained to Nancy that he had left the circus because he could not get along with Reinhold Kroon.

"What has happened since I left the circus, Dan?" he asked.

Webster began with the explanation that Kroon's personality was an odd mixture. He could be the most delightful, charming person one would want to meet. The next moment, he could become hard and cruel.

"The circus folks both admire and hate him," Dan Webster continued. "To some of us, it doesn't make much difference. We do our work and go our way. The circus takes care of you, and if you have a place to sleep and get three meals a day, the rest doesn't count."

"Why do the circus people hate and fear Kroon?" Nancy asked, though she knew of some who had good reason to dislike the ringmaster.

"Well, it's hard to say, Miss Drew. Kroon is one of those people who seems to hypnotize everybody around him. He orders them to do impossible things and somehow or other they do them. Take Lolita for instance. I know that girl well. Actually she's scared to death to get up where it's high, but every time her father insists, she goes ahead and does it. Of course, Lolita is plucky and skilled in her own right, too. Poor girl she's not very happy these days."

Dan Webster went on to say that Sims, who owned the circus, was like a piece of putty in Kroon's hands. Actually the owner took orders from the ringmaster!

"I can't figure it out," the horse trainer said. "It almost seems as if the ringmaster has an evil, uncanny hold over Sims and Lolita, and even Mrs Kroon."

Nancy asked if Mrs Kroon were one of the performers.

"She used to be a bareback rider," Dan Webster replied. "But she got too heavy and had to give it up. Now she just helps her husband and her daughter. Once in a while she speaks up as if she were about to get something off her mind—and man alive! You ought to see the looks her husband gives her. She shuts up like a clam."

Nancy brought the subject around to Lolita and Pietro.

Webster told her that he thought they were romantically interested in each other, but that Kroon would never let his adopted daughter out of his sight.

"So these two young folks don't have a chance to be alone at all," he said. "Between you and me, I'm afraid Kroon and the circus would fold up if Lolita should ever leave."

After a pause, Dan Webster turned to Nancy and asked her if she was game to try another stunt. Just in case he should have to call on her at some time he wanted to make sure that she could do the trick.

"A somersault across the horse's back while it's moving," Webster told her. "Like to give it a try?"

Nancy hesitated for a moment. Then she decided that actually the stunt might not be as difficult as it sounded. The stunt would depend completely on a matter of correct timing. She asked Dan Webster about it.

"You're absolutely right," he said. "Watch the rhythm of the horse's gait. Hum a tune to Belgian Star's slow, rhythmical canter. Then decide exactly from which point you should start to run. When you're sure of your timing, take a few steps towards the horse, put your head and shoulders on the mare's back, and over you go."

Roberto was not sure that even his star pupil should attempt such a trick. Before permitting Nancy to try it, he insisted that she put on a padded jacket and hat in case of a fall. But with precision timing, Nancy did the somersault perfectly.

"Splendid! Splendid!" Webster cried jubilantly.

Just as Nancy was turning a second somersault, Bess and George arrived. George gasped at seeing the stunt, and Bess shrieked. The cry almost made Nancy lose her balance, and Bess apologized profusely for her outburst.

"I wish you'd give up this stunt riding," Bess pleaded fearfully. "You can have just as much fun trotting along."

The others were amused by Bess's remark. Dan Webster did admit, though, that certain people have a natural talent for managing a horse.

"Miss Drew is definitely one of those people," he said, and then announced that he must get back to the circus.

From his pocket Webster pulled out a ticket to the afternoon performance. He handed it to Nancy, suggesting that she come to the show and watch the bareback riding very intently.

"You can pick up lots of pointers," he said. Turning to Bess and George, he added, "Sorry I haven't any more tickets."

"Oh, that's all right," said Bess. "The trapeze stuff scares me, anyway."

Since Nancy's lesson was over, she said goodbye to the cousins and the two men, and started for her car. Upon reaching home, she found Hannah Gruen busy in the kitchen preparing lunch.

"Oh, that looks yummy!" Nancy said, but was interrupted by the doorbell.

As she approached the door, Nancy wondered if the caller might be Pietro.

Opening the door, Nancy saw a young couple she did not recognize. The girl was attractively dressed and wore a hat with a large brim.

"Let us in quickly!" she said, stepping into the hall.

The man looked nervously over his shoulder towards the street.

· 8 ·

Surprising News

As the pretty caller stepped into the Drew home, Nancy suddenly recognized her.

"Lolita!" she cried.

The young man with her smiled as Nancy invited him to enter also.

"I'm sorry I didn't know you at first, Lolita," said Nancy. "You look so different in street clothes."

"And I rarely wear them," the aerialist replied. "As a matter of fact, I borrowed these."

The girl did not explain further, and Nancy wondered if perhaps poor Lolita had no street clothes of her own, since her father rarely let her leave the circus.

It suddenly occurred to Lolita that Nancy did not recognize her escort. Laughing, she said, "I'd like to present my fiancé, Pietro."

Nancy's eyes opened wide. The clown was a very handsome man with features quite different from the garishly painted ones which Nancy remembered from his trick act on the ladder.

"I certainly didn't recognize you, Pietro," she said, smiling. "And what's this about you two being engaged? I think it's wonderful!"

The couple blushed shyly and Lolita confided in Nancy that they had just decided an hour or so before that they would be married as soon as possible.

"There are two obstacles in my way, though," said Lolita, her smile suddenly vanishing. "One is my father. I mean my foster father. He would never consent to my marriage if he heard about it."

"But I'm not going to let that make any difference," Pietro spoke up. "Lolita and I will go to another circus and find work."

Nancy knew that both were excellent performers and any circus would be glad to have them. On the other hand, she recalled what she had heard about Kroon's hold on people. It might prove difficult for the couple to get away from him.

"What is your other problem?" Nancy asked. "Is it about the mystery you asked me to help you with?"

The young aerialist said that she wanted to learn more about her own mother and father before she married. Perhaps she was too sentimental, but if either or both parents were alive, she wanted them to attend her wedding.

"The Kroons never legally adopted me, you know," Lolita explained. "They have just taken it for granted that I belong to them, and it was not until recently that I found out I don't."

"Did the Kroons tell you that?" Nancy questioned.

"Oh, my goodness, no," Lolita answered. "Pietro, suppose you tell the rest of the story."

Nancy had led the way into the living-room and now all three sat down.

"Please tell your story," Nancy urged.

The young man revealed that his father was a retired clown. During his career, he had been with Sims', but before that had performed in Europe with the same circus that the Flying Flanders had.

"So he knew my mother and father," Lolita spoke

up, "and told Pietro that the Kroons never really adopted me."

"According to Mr Kroon," Pietro went on, "Lolita's parents were badly injured during their trapeze act. They were taken to a hospital and died. At that time, the Kroons took Lolita away.

"Just this morning I had a letter from my father, who lives in England, saying he had attended a circus outside the town of Tewkesbury. While looking through a pair of field glasses at the crowd, he had seen a woman he was sure was Lolita's mother."

The clown said his father had hurried towards the woman but she had disappeared before he could reach her. Later, he had inquired in the town but no one he spoke to had ever heard of a Lola Flanders.

"As soon as I read about Lola, I went to Mr Kroon and told him," Pietro said. "I thought he would be glad to hear that Lolita's mother might be alive, but instead he went into a terrible rage. It ended by his telling me to mind my own business, that the whole thing was a lie, and that I could get out of the circus."

"But you're not going to?" Nancy asked.

"Not until Lolita does," the clown replied. "But things are in an awful state. Mr Kroon has even forbidden me to speak to Lolita."

Lolita explained that this was why her fiancé had not appeared in the ring the evening before. She had persuaded him, however, to take part in the show that afternoon.

"The only reason we were able to get away was because Mr Kroon was having a conference with Mr Sims, who has just returned," she explained. "Even so, we thought we were being followed. I think we'd better hurry back, don't you, Pietro?"

A worried frown creased Lolita's forehead.

"I wish you would stay and have luncheon with me," Nancy said.

"Oh, thank you so much, but we wouldn't dare!" the aerialist cried. "My foster father would be sure to discover we'd left the circus. But you'll help me find my mother, won't you?"

"I certainly will," Nancy assured her. "By the way, my father is a lawyer. Suppose he tries to learn what he can through friends in England."

Lolita said that would be wonderful. She hoped Mr Drew would have good news for her.

Before the couple left, Nancy remarked that she expected to attend the afternoon performance in order to get pointers on trick bareback riding. She asked Lolita if it would be possible while she was there for her to talk with Mrs Kroon.

"I don't know," Lolita replied, "but do try, Nancy. She'll probably be in my trailer. Maybe you can find out something from her. She's very nice when my foster father's not around, but she certainly is afraid of him."

"Do you know why?"

"No, I don't. Well, goodbye for now."

Nancy arrived early at the circus and went at once to find Mrs Kroon. On purpose the young detective wore her new charm bracelet and made a point of jingling it as she introduced herself to the ringmaster's wife. Although Mrs Kroon eyed the bracelet, she made no comment.

"I'm interested in circus riding," Nancy said. "I understand that you used to perform in the circus yourself."

"That's right," Mrs Kroon said, but offered no further information.

"Did your daughter Lolita inherit her talent from you?" Nancy asked.

Instantly Mrs Kroon's expression changed from one of pleasantness to fear, then anger. Instead of replying, she said:

"How did you get in here? Visitors aren't allowed in this section. Our private lives are our own business. I shan't answer any questions and I'll thank you to leave at once!"

"Oh, I'm sorry," Nancy said. "Perhaps I am a little too curious. Please forgive me."

"You're more than that," Mrs Kroon fairly screamed. "You're a nuisance."

Nancy decided not to press the irate woman further and backed out of the trailer. She noticed that several circus performers were standing around, listening. At first she was embarrassed, but a remark one of the onlookers made put her at ease.

"Don't mind Mrs Kroon," a woman said in a low voice. "Her bark is worse than her bite. Lolita's her adopted daughter and she's awful touchy on the subject."

"I see," said Nancy.

She started off but changed her mind. Coming back, she asked the woman:

"Are Lolita's own parents living?"

The woman exchanged glances with the other performers standing close by. Finally she said:

"I may as well tell you. There's a story going around that Lolita's real mother is alive and that the Kroons don't want anybody to know this. Personally, we think there's something very strange about the whole thing."

Nancy asked if the woman could give her any further details. But at this moment the group of performers saw the ringmaster approaching and hurried out of sight.

Nancy herself turned the corner rather abruptly to avoid meeting the man. She hurried off to the big top and found her seat. It was alongside one of the entrance aisles.

As she waited for the show to begin, Nancy mulled over the various angles of the mystery. Had Lola Flanders pawned the bracelet? And why? Was she the person who needed help? Were the Kroons at the back of her trouble?

Nancy was brought out of her reverie by the band striking up. Presently the parade started. This and the act of the clowns interested her as much as it had at the first performance. Pietro waved to her. Many of the performers seemed to recognize her and nodded. She felt as if they were all becoming friends of hers.

Nancy paid particular attention to the first bare-back riding act. As Dan Webster had suggested, she noted the horses' rhythms and found that the riders were experts at timing themselves to the movements whether they were standing on the animals' backs, running, or somersaulting. One of the attractive girl riders seemed very young. But she was more proficient than the others and did a great deal of solo work while the older ones stood by.

The young rider had just completed a mid-air double somersault and landed on the horse's back, amid tumultuous applause, when an object came whizzing through the air and hit the horse on the nose. The mare reared and bucked, throwing the young rider.

At once there was great confusion among the riders and their frightened horses. In the midst of it, Nancy spotted something familiar lying on the ground—the object which had struck the horse.

Nancy gasped. It was a whip exactly like the one which her assailant had used!

· 9 ·

Meeting a Challenge

THE injured bareback rider tried to stand, but it was evident at once that her ankle was either badly sprained or broken. Her face was creased with pain as she put an arm round the shoulders of two men riders who helped her from the ring. Meanwhile, her horse had run to the exit.

The remaining performers carried on, doing their best, but it was evident that the mishap had made them nervous. At a signal from the band, evidently inspired by Kroon, the act came to an abrupt end.

The whip which had caused the accident had been kicked out of the way and seemed to have been forgotten by everyone but Nancy. She assumed that the performers thought some child had thrown it. The young sleuth herself was becoming confused.

"I thought the person who tried to strangle me had it in for me personally," she mused. "But what could have been his motive for injuring the circus rider?"

Recalling her first suspicions of the stableman at Roberto's riding academy, Nancy wondered if it was possible that Hitch had perpetrated all three bits of mischief.

"Hitch did warn me not to do any circus riding," Nancy reminded herself. "Maybe he doesn't want other girls to, either."

As the next act was being announced, Nancy saw Chief of Police McGinnis of the River Heights force walk into the box which she had occupied the evening before. He was wearing civilian clothes. Getting up, she hurried over and seated herself beside him.

"Hello, Nancy," he said genially. "What's the mystery this time? Whenever you seek me out, I know something's in the wind!"

Nancy smiled and confessed that she did have a problem. She asked if he had reached the circus in time to see what had happened to the young bareback rider.

"No," the chief replied, "but the guard outside told me about the accident. Too bad. I was hoping the circus would get through their three days here without any trouble. But I suppose we have to expect such things."

"It's my idea," Nancy said thoughtfully, "that it was a deliberate attempt to injure the girl and her horse."

"What makes you think so?" the officer asked.

Nancy told him what had happened to her the evening before with the very same kind of whip.

The chief whistled. "Why didn't you tell me before now what happened to you?" he demanded.

Nancy explained that Ned had spoken to the circus policeman.

"And we did make a search for the man," Nancy replied.

Chief McGinnis, who admired Nancy's prowess as a detective, remarked, "Since you couldn't find the man, it was probably because he skipped out."

"I also had a threatening note from the strangler," Nancy went on. "I was going to bring it to you, but so many things have happened since then that I had no chance. I did look it over carefully, Chief, and couldn't find a clue to the writer."

"Well," he said, smiling, "we'll call your findings the preliminary investigation. You bring the note to headquarters. I'd like to give it a microscopic test."

Nancy promised to do so, then told Chief McGinnis of her suspicions about Hitch. After she mentioned the stableman's warning to her about stunt riding and the incident of the stone throwing, the officer advised Nancy to be wary.

"I certainly think that you have good reason for suspecting that fellow Hitch," he said. "I'll put a watch on him right away."

Nancy returned to her seat and concentrated on Lolita's act. The performance went off exceedingly well. As it ended, and Nancy was adding her applause to that of the enthusiastic crowd, an usher came up to her with a note.

It was from Dan Webster, asking her to meet him in his office at once.

"Something very important has come up," the note said.

Nancy got up and hurried from the tent. A hundred thoughts flashed through her mind before she reached the office. What could he want of her? As she walked in, Dan Webster smiled and offered her a chair. Then, looking directly at her, he said:

"I won't beat around the bush, Miss Drew. I want you to take the place of that injured bare-back rider."

Nancy was so amazed she opened her mouth and

closed it again without speaking. Then she managed to exclaim:

"You want me to take that girl's place!"

"I told you this morning, Miss Drew, that you ride well enough to be in the circus."

"But I can't perform like that girl!" Nancy objected. "She's excellent. By the way, how is she?"

Webster revealed that the young rider's ankle had been broken in the fall. It was questionable whether she would ever be able to perform the act again. "Oh, what a shame!" Nancy cried, then added, "Thank you for your compliment, Mr Webster, but really I'll have to refuse. Even if I could do the riding, I know Mr Kroon would never approve of my joining Sims' Circus."

The horse trainer said he did not think the ringmaster would disapprove. Furthermore, Kroon had given an ultimatum that the bareback act was to be filled in before the evening show or the whole troupe would be dismissed.

"The performers might change their routine, but unfortunately the horses can't," Webster told her. "It takes a long time to train them and there's no changing 'em."

Nancy felt sorry for the group that depended on the act for their livelihood. If she could ride for one or two performances, until they found a replacement, it might help.

Dan Webster took her silence as a sign of refusal. Leaning towards her, he said in a whisper:

"Miss Drew, this might be your golden opportunity to solve the mystery of the circus. If you lived with us for a week or so, you could watch the Kroons at close range."

This plea did the trick. Laughing, Nancy said that

she would join the circus, provided her father approved.

"He's on a trip, but I'll try to locate him," she promised. "I'm not sure where he is staying at present."

Dan Webster pushed the telephone towards Nancy and insisted that she begin calling. First she tried Mr Drew's office, only to learn that they had not heard from him that day and did not know where he was.

As she put down the phone, Lolita and Pietro walked into the office. Nancy was surprised to see them together, and Lolita must have guessed her thoughts.

"We're becoming very bold being seen with each other." The circus star laughed happily.

Pietro frowned. "But look for an explosion if Mr Kroon sees us!"

"Let's not worry," the aerialist said, and added that all her friends in the circus were acting as lookouts and would notify the couple at once if Lolita's foster father were close by.

"Say," Dan Webster spoke up, "you two will have to help me out. Nancy Drew must take the place of Rosa. I have persuaded her, but she tells me she won't join the circus unless her father gives permission, and we can't locate Mr Drew. What am I going to do?"

Lolita walked over to Nancy and put an arm round the girl. "I think it would be nice for you to have your father's permission, she said, "but, after all, he doesn't object to your doing the circus riding at Señor Roberto's?"

"No."

"Then what's the difference whether you're riding in our ring or the one at the riding academy?" Lolita asked persuasively.

"I don't suppose there is any," Nancy agreed, "but I'd still like to get in touch with him. I have an idea.

Two friends of mine who often work on mysteries with me will be glad to try to locate him, I'm sure. In the meantime, I'll practise some stunt riding. After all," she reminded the others, "I haven't ridden with the other members of the bareback troupe. The whole thing might be a flop with me in it."

Dan Webster said that the equestrian group were meeting in twenty minutes to decide what to do about the act. If Nancy would come to the main tent at that time, he would introduce her and let them see her work

"I'll find you some riding clothes, Nancy," Lolita offered. "Come on!"

Before leaving the office, Nancy telephoned to Bess and George, who, she knew, were at Roberto's academy. They were overwhelmed to hear that their friend planned to ride in the circus. Bess begged Nancy to reconsider, but finally she promised to help locate Mr Drew.

Nancy and Lolita left Webster's office with Pietro. They had gone only a few steps when one of the midgets rushed up to Lolita.

"Your father's coming!" he warned her.

With that, Pietro dodged behind a truck. The two girls went on. A moment later they were confronted by Kroon.

"Who is this, Lolita?" he asked sternly. Giving Nancy a piercing look, he asked, "Aren't you the girl who let that kid sneak a ride in Cinderella's carriage during the parade?"

The ringmaster did not wait for Nancy to answer. His eyes flashing, he ordered her to leave the circus grounds at once. Then, turning to Lolita, he snapped:

"Get to your trailer and don't come out until supper-time!"

Over Kroon's shoulder, Nancy could see Pietro beckoning to her. His sign language seemed to indicate that she was to pretend to leave and that he would follow and meet her later. After bidding Lolita goodbye, Nancy started off. Kroon stood there until he was sure his daughter had obeyed his command, then he stalked away.

A short distance farther on, Pietro caught up to Nancy. He offered to guide her to the trailer where extra costumes were kept, including riding habits.

Nancy shook her head. "It wouldn't be safe now, Pietro. I suspect that Mr Kroon knows who I am and that I have solved mysteries. I think he referred to Teddy as an excuse for ordering me to leave. He doesn't want me around here and will do anything to keep me away."

Pietro looked crestfallen. After a moment of silence, he said, "Even so, Nancy, you must stay and see what you can do for Lolita and me. Listen! I'm going to tell you something that I don't even dare tell my fiancée. She would be worried sick.

"I was walking past Mr and Mrs Kroon's trailer a little while ago. I believe they thought nobody was around. Mrs Kroon was crying and saying to her husband:

" 'The money won't do us any good if people find out where it came from.' "

Nancy was startled. "Have you any idea what Mrs Kroon meant?" she asked the clown, but he shook his head.

Nancy's mind jumped to a possible conclusion. The Kroons might have secretly gained possession of money which did not rightfully belong to them!

· 10 ·

A Quick Switch

THERE was no question now in Nancy Drew's mind that if she consented to riding in the circus act she would be undertaking something dangerous—not only dangerous from the angle of riding, but intuition told her there would be other hazards, too.

If Kroon were a dishonest as well as a sinister character, he would not let a girl like Nancy stop him from gaining his own ends. And if Kroon had learned that she was an amateur sleuth, he might use more drastic means to keep her from interfering.

"Please don't let us down," Pietro pleaded once more. "You see what a dreadful position Lolita is in. Even if we ran away and were married, I don't believe it would solve our problem. Kroon might continue to make life miserable for us."

"I agree," Nancy answered. "I'll do everything I can for you and Lolita. But if my father disapproves of my living at the circus I'll have to do my detective work on the outside."

"I understand," Pietro said and thanked her. Then he took Nancy to Mrs Kelly, the wardrobe mistress. The girl was quickly outfitted in dark-blue jodhpurs and a white silk blouse. But instead of boots she was given soft, heel-less slippers.

Ready to leave the trailer, she glanced at Mrs Kelly's wrist watch.

"The twenty minutes are almost up," she thought. "I'll have to hurry."

Dan Webster was waiting for her inside the big top. He introduced the equestrian group and their leader, Rancoco.

"Erika here," said Dan, taking the arm of a girl rider, "will be your room-mate when you join us."

Erika was a very attractive young woman with lovely blonde hair and big, blue eyes. She smiled at Nancy, saying:

"I thought I might give you some pointers when we're alone, but from what Dan tells me, I doubt that you'll need any."

"I'm afraid Dan has built me up too much," Nancy said. "But I'll do my best. What's first?"

Fortunately for the act, the lead horse, whose nose had been bruised, was all right otherwise and able to perform. She was the same size and build as Belgian Star, so when Nancy swung herself to the mare's back, she almost felt as if she were riding Roberto's thoroughbred.

Despite this, Nancy was a trifle tense. At first she went through the stunts rather stiffly, but when Erika reminded her to relax, the performance went much better.

Not only did Nancy show the onlookers the riding tricks Roberto had taught her, but she tried to imitate the girl who had been injured. The group of equestrians was enthusiastic.

"Well, what do you think?" Dan asked Rancoco.

"For a girl not reared in the circus, Miss Drew is remarkable," the leader replied. "Even if she can't join us permanently, I'd certainly be glad to take her on for a few days until we can get a replacement for Rosa."

Nancy was glad to hear the equestrian's decision. She had just about decided that everything was turning out well when Pietro came racing into the tent, greatly agitated.

"Kroon's coming! He suspects something funny is going on. He's in a fearful rage and says he's going to dismiss all of you for double-crossing him!"

The riders were stunned and asked what the ringmaster meant. They had done no harm and yet in a few moments every one of them might be out of a job!

Nancy was sure that the trouble centred around her. Somehow, Kroon had found out that the young detective might join the circus. This did not suit his plans.

"Pietro, he must have found out about me," Nancy whispered to the clown.

Pietro's face was dark with anger. "I'm afraid so. Nancy, there's a spy in this big top and I'm going to find out who he is!"

Before the clown could carry out his threat, Bess Marvin rushed into the tent. Seeing her in riding clothes gave Nancy an idea. Without waiting to hear why Bess had come, Nancy said to her quickly:

"Kroon's coming in here any minute. He must have heard I'm trying out for a part in this act. He mustn't see me. You'll have to take my place!"

Nancy gave poor Bess no time to make a choice. Nancy dived behind some of the seats, just as the ringmaster walked in. He strode over to Bess.

"So you're the girl who's trying out, eh?"

"Why—uh, yes," Bess replied.

"I thought somebody else was," he said. Then, with a grunt, he added, "You don't look much like a rider. Well, get up on the mare and let's see what you can do."

Obediently Bess climbed up. She felt sick with fear

and only her affection and loyalty for Nancy gave her the courage to carry on.

Bess rode well and Kroon seemed to be impressed. But presently he called, "Now let's see what stunts you can do."

Bess's heart thumped wildly. What should she do?

"Oh, please, not in these clothes," Bess stammered. "I—that is—could you come back in an hour, Mr Kroon?"

"An hour!" the ringmaster yelled. "You want an hour to change your clothes? That's nonsense. I'll give you exactly half—well, forty-five minutes," he said.

"Oh, thank you," Bess said, sliding from the horse.

Kroon looked at Rancoco. "I want every one of you back here in exactly forty-five minutes. I'll be here to watch the act. If I don't like it, out you go. This time I won't change my mind!"

As he stalked off, there was silence. The equestrians were too worried to talk, and Nancy realized how much depended on her. As the girl emerged from behind the seats, Bess ran to Nancy and begged her not to take part in the bareback riders' act.

"You're just going to get yourself into trouble," Bess insisted. "And it isn't worth the risk."

"I couldn't let these people down now," Nancy replied. "And thanks a million for helping me. By the way," she said, taking off the charm bracelet, "will you give this to Hannah?"

"Glad to," Bess replied.

"Bess, did you find my dad?" Nancy asked.

"No and yes."

Bess reported that George had contacted Nancy's Aunt Eloise Drew in New York City. Aunt Eloise was expecting her brother at any moment and would have him telephone George's home as soon as he arrived. Bess had dashed to the circus to tell Nancy.

"Oh, I do hope Dad won't object to my appearing in the circus!" Nancy said.

"Well, I just hope he does," Bess declared.

"Is George at home now?" Nancy asked.

"Yes."

As Bess continued to tell her friend how worried she was, Nancy suddenly laughed.

"You know what's worrying me the most at this moment?" she asked. "How I'm going to fool Kroon into thinking I'm Bess Marvin!"

Erika, who overheard the remark, smiled. "It won't be any trouble at all," she said. "Our make-up artist can fix that. And you must have a blonde rinse," she went on, looking at Bess, "and a short haircut. Then with some rouge on your cheeks—you'll fool Mr Kroon all right!"

"Let's get started," Nancy urged.

The three girls went off together, and within half an hour Nancy's appearance was considerably changed.

"You could pass for Bess's thinner sister at a short distance," Erika told her, adding that Kroon probably would not notice the slight difference in proportions.

As the girls left the make-up artist's tent, they almost bumped into George Fayne. She stared at Nancy as if she had seen a ghost.

"What's been going on?" she exclaimed.

Quickly George was brought up to date on the news, then Nancy asked, "Did my father telephone?"

George said he had. She grinned and said that Mr Drew would be very happy to let Nancy perform in the circus act. His daughter breathed a sigh of relief, and George added:

"What's more, your aunt is flying up with him from New York to see the evening performance."

Nancy was pleased! She would do her very best—that is, if she could pass Kroon's inspection. So much depended on her now. She must not fail!

· 11 ·

A Ruse Works

It suddenly occurred to Nancy that she had told Hannah Gruen she would be home at six o'clock and it was now six-thirty. Since Bess had not gone there yet with the bracelet, and told her of Nancy's plans, the housekeeper would be worried. Nancy decided to call her at once.

"I'll invite her to the evening performance," Nancy thought, her eyes dancing. "But I'll keep my part in it as a surprise!"

The housekeeper answered the telephone.

"Hello, Hannah," Nancy said. "I'm still at the circus. I hope you haven't been worrying about me."

Mrs Gruen said indeed she had been. A very important message had come for Nancy an hour before.

"Chief McGinnis called and left a message for you," she reported. "That fellow Hitch has disappeared. You're to watch your step!"

The news disturbed Nancy. She felt sure that the

stableman had run away because he was guilty of the three suspicious incidents which had occurred.

"Did the chief tell you anything else?" Nancy asked the housekeeper.

"Yes, he did. One of his men found some souvenir whips hidden in Hitch's quarters. And furthermore, he told me that Hitch had tried to strangle you. Oh, Nancy, you must be careful. That fellow's clothes are still at the stable, which means he's probably still around here. There's no telling what that madman may try next."

Nancy was worried, too. It occurred to her that very possibly Hitch was lurking around the circus grounds, planning more devilry. If he were, nobody would be safe.

Aloud Nancy said, "Don't think anything more about it, Hannah. Let's talk about something more pleasant. I'm staying at the circus and having supper with Lolita. Isn't that thrilling?"

"I suppose so," the housekeeper replied, "but don't you get any fancy ideas, Nancy Drew, about becoming an aerialist. It's bad enough that you're doing that stunt riding."

Nancy laughed, then told Hannah that she was staying for the evening performance and very much wanted her to come.

"Dad will be here," she said gaily, "and someone else you like very much. We'll make it a party!"

Hannah promised to attend and asked about a ticket. Nancy told her that she would leave one at the ticket booth. After completing the telephone conversation, Nancy went at once to find Dan Webster. He was pleased to hear that she had her father's approval and promised to have Box AA set aside for the family's use.

When Nancy told him about Hitch and her suspicions

that he might be hiding in the circus grounds, Dan's face became livid with anger. "Why that shrivelled-up, good-for-nothing!" he shouted. "I never did have any use for him when he was with Sims', and now I have less than ever. I'll find him! He won't get away with another one of his tricks!"

Telling Nancy to go ahead to the big tent, the horse trainer hurried off to instigate a search. Relieved, she hurried back to where she had left Bess. Nancy took her arm as the girls went to the riding ring.

The equestrian group was there and complimented Nancy on her appearance.

"Oh, I do hope I can fool Mr Kroon," she said. Turning to Rancoco, Nancy added, "Will you do something for me?"

"Yes, Nancy. What is it?"

She suggested that the ringmaster be kept at a distance, so that he would have no chance to detect the substitution.

"I'm sure I can arrange it," Rancoco said. "Here comes Kroon now. I'll speak to him."

To Nancy's delight, Rancoco was able to persuade the ringmaster to remain at a distance by telling him that he should view the act as though he were part of the audience.

"All right," the man's voice boomed across the empty tent, as he sat down in one of the boxes. "Now get to work! And make it snappy! I've got too much work to be hanging around here."

Rancoco hurried across the ring and the act started. Nancy was determined to do her part with precision. And the members of the troupe were equally bent upon helping her as much as possible.

Everything went smoothly. One of the men riders

added an intricate solo of his own to take the place of one of Rosa's specialities.

Kroon seemed pleased, and for a few minutes he seemed like a different person—a very handsome, affable man. But presently he became as harsh and brutal as usual.

"This will do for a week or so," he shouted. "But, Rancoco, see to it that your girl soloist gets back in. Men performers are all right, but an audience likes to see girl riders do the tricky things."

After Kroon had left the tent, Bess came out of hiding. She heaved a big sigh and said to Nancy:

"Well, I'm glad that's over! I suppose there's no talking you out of the performance, but I certainly am worried."

Nancy put an arm around her friend. "This may surprise you, Bess," she said, "but the trick riding is almost getting to be automatic with me. Really, it doesn't seem hard at all."

Bess stared at her, not sure whether Nancy really meant it or whether she was just trying to make her feel better. She said no more about it, however, and asked if Nancy were coming home now.

"No, I'm staying here for supper," she said.

After telling Bess there would be seats for her and George in Box AA, Nancy said goodbye.

Lolita had asked Nancy to meet her at the cafeteria. The aerialist had told her that suppertime was the only period when she was permitted to be with her friends in the circus.

Nancy hoped Pietro might join their little group. But when she mentioned this, Lolita told her that Kroon had someone watching her.

"I understand he asked one of the midgets to keep an

eye on me. Oh, Nancy," Lolita wailed, "it's dreadful to have your father set spies on you."

The young detective thought how wonderful it would be if either or both of Lolita's own parents were alive, and she could find them and give Lolita a happy life. What a wonderful reunion it would be!

Then suddenly it occurred to Nancy that Kroon might have a good reason for keeping the Flanders hidden. To Lolita she said presently:

"Did your own parents leave any money in trust for you?"

"Oh, I don't think so. Mr Kroon never mentioned it and I'm sure he would have told me."

Nancy was not so sure of this, in view of what Pietro had overheard Mrs Kroon say to her husband.

At this moment she saw Dan Webster making his way towards her, a worried look on his face. He reported to Nancy that the circus grounds had been thoroughly searched but no one had found any sign of Hitch.

Lolita grabbed Nancy's hand. "What's all this about?" she demanded. After hearing the story, the aerialist leaned towards Dan Webster and said, "Oh, nothing must happen to Nancy! I'd never forgive myself!"

"I agree with you a hundred per cent, Lolita," Dan replied. "This whole thing has me very much upset."

As he finished speaking, a gong sounded in the cafeteria tent. Dan said that it was a signal for all the performers to leave and return to their quarters to get ready for the evening performance.

Nancy's heart began to thump wildly. Up to this moment she had not fully realized that she was actually part of the circus. Soon she would be under the floodlights performing for hundreds of people!

"I must hurry and try on my costume," Nancy told herself.

She walked towards the trailer where earlier she had made a date with Mrs Kelly, the wardrobe mistress.

"I'm all ready for you," the woman said pleasantly. "This is poor Rosa's costume. Suppose you try on the dress and we'll see how it fits."

Nancy removed her riding habit and stepped into the white satin, ballerina-skirted costume. It fitted perfectly!

A few minutes later Nancy was completely outfitted. Carrying the costume and accessories over her arm, she set off for Erika's tent, where the two girls would dress and then go to the make-up artist.

The young bareback rider was just turning a corner past the supply tent when she remembered that she had no cream to remove her make-up. She went inside to purchase a jar. Laying the costume on a chair near the open doorway, Nancy looked round for someone to attend her. No one was there.

She waited several minutes. Interested in the various items, Nancy walked about, getting farther and farther from the door. When still no one came, she decided to leave.

As the young detective turned around, she found herself looking straight at the missing stableman! Hitch had her costume in his hands and was about to run off with it.

"Stop!" Nancy cried, dashing across the supply tent.

But by the time she reached the doorway Hitch was out of sight!

· 12 ·

A Dangerous Performance

NANCY had to get back her costume! It was the only one of its kind in the circus and she needed the fancy riding habit for the evening performance!

None of the circus people were in sight at the moment. With nothing but a hunch to follow, Nancy chose a direction which led to the nearest exit from the circus grounds. But she reached it without discovering her quarry.

Retracing her steps, Nancy started for another exit. As she ran, the young bareback rider began to wonder what she would do if the costume were not found.

"If I have to wear another one, Kroon will be sure to single me out," Nancy thought worriedly. "That will end my riding with the Vascon troupe."

Seeing a workman taking down one of the small tents, Nancy hastened over to him and asked if he had seen a man running from the supply tent.

"No, miss," he replied. "You looking for someone?"

Quickly Nancy told him that she was looking for a man named Hitch.

"Oh, I know him. He used to be connected with the circus."

"He took my costume and I need it," Nancy explained quickly. "Please help me find Hitch and hold him for the police."

"I'll do my best, miss," the workman promised, hurrying away to help in the search.

Nancy decided to appeal to Dan Webster and went to his office. The horse trainer was thunderstruck when she told him of the groom's latest bit of devilry, and blamed himself.

"I thought we searched every part of these grounds for Hitch," he said, "and all guards at the entrances were warned not to let him in or out."

"I know you did your best," Nancy said. "Right now, I must get my costume back. If Hitch has left the circus grounds and taken it with him, I don't know what I'll do."

Dan Webster picked up his telephone. He called the ticket office and every other person stationed on the outside of the grounds. The last guard to whom he phoned said:

"Hey, wait a minute! I see something."

A moment later the man reported that he had the missing costume.

"It was in a box under one of the booths. I noticed a man put a package down there, but didn't know he was Hitch."

At the time the guard had not given the incident a second thought, and did not know where Hitch had gone.

"I'm sure he didn't leave the grounds, though," the guard reported.

Dan asked him to bring the costume at once to his office. While they were waiting for it, he warned Nancy to be wary every minute until the groom was caught.

When the costume arrived, Nancy found to her relief that it was intact.

Hitch had evidently grabbed up a large box from the

supply tent and put the costume and accessories into it so that he would not be spotted with them.

"Oh, thanks so much," Nancy said to Dan, and hurried off to join Erika to dress for the performance.

"My goodness, where have you been?" her roommate asked. "It's only fifteen minutes to parade time!"

Nancy told her what had happened. Erika was aghast. "I hope that awful man left the circus grounds," she said as she helped Nancy into her costume. Then the two girls raced to the make-up artist's tent.

Nancy was worried. "Will I have to pass Kroon's inspection in the parade?"

She was greatly relieved when Erika said that the ringmaster never bothered to view the parades. The girls had just received their last fluffs of face powder when the warning gong sounded. They hurried off and swung on to the backs of their mounts. The band struck up, and a moment later the parade started.

Nancy had never been more excited and nervous in her life. Not only was it thrilling to be riding with the circus people, but a fear lurked in her mind that Hitch, still at large, might be hiding close by, ready to harm her or one of the other riders.

As Nancy came opposite the box where her father and Aunt Eloise were seated, she noticed to her delight that Hannah, Bess, George, and Ned were there also. They waved to her, but Nancy did not dare acknowledge the greeting. Kroon or one of his spies might be watching.

Finally the parade was over and the clown act began. As soon as they had finished their performance, Ringmaster Kroon entered the ring to announce the equestrian act.

The group of horses trotted in and took their places

in the ring. The performance started, the mares cantering about rhythmically to the music. Singly, and together, the riders did their stunts.

In Box AA Mr Drew and his friends gripped the arms of their chairs, their eyes riveted on Nancy. They could scarcely believe that she was actually a bareback rider in Sims' Circus!

Nancy outdid herself. She made no mistakes and her performance was the best she had ever given. When Rancoco jumped up behind her on the mare and they cantered round the ring, he whispered enthusiastically:

"Superb, Miss Drew, superb!"

Pleased, Nancy smiled. The show went on without interruption. But just as one of the men riders began his solo number, there was a wild scream in the audience.

Turning, the equestrians saw a hard-thrown baseball whizzing from one of the exits directly at them!

The warning cry saved them from injury. Like lightning, each performer pulled his horse to the ground and lay down himself. The speeding ball sailed over their heads and landed beyond the ring.

The audience was divided in its reaction. Some were stunned. But many people thought it was part of the act and clapped loudly.

Their attitude helped to steady the nerves of the performers whose knees were shaking. They recovered themselves instantly and the performance went on.

Out of the corner of her eye, Nancy could see a commotion in the exit. Men were running after someone. Without being told, she was sure that the ball-throwing incident had been another of Hitch's unwarranted acts of malicious mischief.

As soon as she and Erika reached their dressing room,

Nancy announced that she was changing to street clothes.

"Where are you going?" her room-mate asked.

"I'm not sure," Nancy said, "but first, I'm going to the box where my father is."

Erika warned her that she must be back for the finale because Kroon was always on hand for the closing pageant. Though he did not particularly notice the faces of each individual performer, he never failed to take a count of the number. If anyone was missing, his wrath was aroused.

"Please don't let anything go wrong that might endanger our troupe," she begged.

"I won't," Nancy promised. "Just how much time will there be before the final number?"

Erika glanced at the clock. "Two and a half hours."

"I'll be back in time," said Nancy, and left the dressing-room.

She asked Dan Webster whether the ball thrower had been captured and was told that he had escaped.

"It probably was Hitch," the horse trainer said ruefully. "He's still at large."

Waiting until the ringmaster was busy making an announcement, Nancy made her way to Box AA. Mr Drew and the others greeted her with open arms and whispered that she had been a sensation.

Nancy slid into an empty seat beside Ned. She whispered that she would like him to accompany her on a little sleuthing expedition.

"Of course," Ned replied. "Where to?"

"Roberto's stables," she said, and told him about the missing stableman. "Hitch's clothes are still at the place. He may be hiding there."

Nancy whispered to her father that she and Ned

would be gone for a short time and not to worry about them. She borrowed Mr Drew's ticket so that she might re-enter the circus grounds without any questions being asked.

She and Ned set off. He had brought his car and it took only a few minutes to reach the riding academy.

She asked Ned to park a short distance away from the stable so that they might approach without being seen or heard. The couple were half-way to the rear entrance when Nancy suddenly grabbed her escort's arm.

"Listen!" she said. "Did you hear a door squeak?"

"Yes, I did. Maybe it was only the wind."

The next moment, they heard hoofbeats and frightened whinnies. Nancy became tense.

"That sounds like Belgian Star!" she said excitedly. "Ned, I'm afraid someone is trying to steal her!"

▪ 13 ▪

A Whirlwind Chase

NANCY and Ned raced across the field at the rear of the riding academy. But the mysterious rider already had a good start. In the dim light of evening they caught a brief glimpse of horse and rider disappearing down the road.

"Oh, I'm sure that was Belgian Star!" Nancy cried.

"But what makes you think she was being stolen?"

Ned questioned. "Someone from here may just have been riding off on her."

Nancy shook her head. She explained that if the horse had felt friendly to her rider she would not have whinnied.

Ned suggested that they investigate to see if the mare was really gone. Nancy consented and led the way to the stable. The door squeaked protestingly as she opened it and turned on a light. From where they stood, the two could see that Belgian's Star's stall was empty.

"I guess you're right," said Ned. "What say we take off after that fellow in the car?"

"Yes, let's do," Nancy agreed. "Come on!"

Ned turned the car round and started down the road. They drove nearly a mile before they began to hear the pounding hoofbeats.

The rider must have guessed that he was being pursued. Reaching an open field, he veered abruptly and raced along the edge of it.

Ned made a sharp turn into the field and took off after the rider.

Apparently there was no longer any doubt in the mind of the fleeing rider that he was being trailed, for he made another sharp turn and raced directly across the field.

Ned did the same. But the ground, having been ploughed recently, was soft and rutted.

But Ned drove on doggedly until he came to a brook with a thick wood on the other side.

"Now we can't go any farther," Nancy said, as Ned turned off the engine. She climbed out of the car and called at the top of her voice:

"Star! Whoa! Belgian Star! Whoa! Come back!"

The mare must have heard Nancy, for the hoofbeats and crashing of underbrush stopped.

"Ned, have you a flashlight?" Nancy asked.

"Yes, in the glove compartment."

She ran back to the car and reached into the compartment. At that moment the horse whinnied. Again Nancy cried out:

"Star! Come back!"

Grabbing the flashlight, Nancy turned it on and held the light high in the air. She waved it back and forth, and kept calling to the horse. Suddenly there was a sound of hoofbeats and a frantic trampling of undergrowth. A moment later the car's headlights picked up the oncoming horse. It was Belgian Star with Hitch, the groom, astride her!

At the bank of the brook, the mare stopped. Hitch was straining on the bridle so tightly that the horse's head, with mouth wide open and teeth bared, was lifted towards the sky.

"I'll get this guy!" Ned yelled, and waded into the stream.

In desperation, Hitch jumped from Belgian Star and started off through the woods. Ned was only a few feet behind. Reaching the opposite shore, he plunged into the wood after his quarry.

Belgian Star slowly crossed the stream and came to stand at Nancy's side. The mare nuzzled the girl's neck, as if looking for sympathy. Nancy was stroking the horse when she heard a scream.

"Oh, one of the men has been injured!" she thought fearfully.

Quickly mounting the mare, Nancy urged her across the stream and into the woods. She started calling Ned's name. There was no answer. Fear clutched her.

Playing the flashlight around, she rode among the trees. A few minutes later, to her complete amazement, she saw both Ned and Hitch lying unconscious in a small clearing.

Dismounting, Nancy rushed to Ned's side first. He was beginning to revive. Nancy chafed his wrists and forehead, and presently he opened his eyes.

"Ned, I'm so thankful you're all right," Nancy said, helping him to sit up.

"Where's Hitch?" he asked immediately.

"Right here," Nancy replied, and pointed to the unconscious stableman.

When she turned the light on Hitch she could see that he had not suffered any serious injuries. He had merely blacked out.

"What happened?" Nancy asked Ned.

He told her that the two had grappled in the darkness. Hitch was clutching the boy's throat, but just before Ned blacked out, he had landed a knockout wallop on Hitch's jaw. Evidently they both had lost consciousness at the same time.

"That guy's a fighter," Ned remarked.

They swung the man's unconscious form across the back of the horse, then they started back through the woods. Nancy led Belgian Star, while Ned watched the prisoner for signs of regaining consciousness.

When they reached the car, Nancy and Ned held a short consultation. They concluded that if they put Hitch in the car, and Nancy rode the horse, the man might revive and try to overpower Ned.

"Do you think Belgian Star could carry two men?" Ned asked.

"It won't hurt her for a short distance."

"Then I suggest," said Ned, "that you drive

the car and I'll ride with this fellow."

Nancy concurred, and Ned and his prisoner went ahead. Just before reaching the riding academy, Hitch began to regain consciousness. Fortunately, he did not become completely coherent until after Ned had carried him inside and laid him on the floor. Together, Nancy and Ned securely tied their prisoner with pieces of harness.

They had just finished when Hitch fully regained consciousness. He tried to sit up but found that he could not do so because of the straps that bound him. Screaming like a madman, he cried out that he had done nothing and they had no business to tie him up.

"Hitch," said Ned, "you have plenty to account for. You'd better start talking."

The groom insisted that he would reveal nothing about himself, except to say that he was merely borrowing Belgian Star to get somewhere.

"You needn't tell us if you don't want to," Nancy said. "You can give your story to the police."

She walked off, heading for a pay telephone which hung on the wall. Since she had no coins, Nancy called to Ned to bring her some.

"I'll call Chief McGinnis for you," he offered. "See if you can get anything out of Hitch."

Returning to the prisoner, Nancy asked him why he had tried to strangle her with the whip at the circus.

The man's eyes nearly bulged from his head. "How'd you know I did that?" he asked.

Nancy did not reply. Instead she asked, "You know the police are looking for you. If you had no reason to run away, why did you leave Roberto's employment?"

"I don't have to work here if I don't want to," Hitch said stubbornly.

"Did you have any reason for throwing the stone at me and injuring the rider at the circus, except that you don't like people to do trick riding?" Nancy questioned the man.

"I ain't talkin'."

Ned returned in a few moments. He told Nancy that Chief McGinnis himself was coming out to the riding academy to take charge of Hitch. While waiting for his arrival, Nancy and Ned discussed the case. Presently Ned remarked:

"I'm surprised that a stable with such valuable horses as these would be left unguarded."

"You're right," said Nancy. "Roberto has an apartment upstairs, you know. He must be away."

The more Nancy thought about this, the more she became convinced that Roberto would not leave the stable unguarded. If we were going to absent himself, he would arrange for some friend to stay there.

"Ned," she said, "I'm worried. Would you mind going upstairs? I'd like to be sure that Roberto is not here."

Ned looked at her, reading the ominous thought in her mind. Without answering, he clicked on a first floor light and dashed up a pair of narrow stairs which led from the stable. A moment later he cried out:

"Nancy, come up here quick!"

·14·

The Clue in the Scrapbook

THE sight that met Nancy's eyes as she reached the first floor of the academy made her wince. On the floor lay Señor Roberto, bound and gagged!

He wore no shirt and across his chest, as well as his face and neck, were a series of red, angry welts. Apparently he had been cruelly whipped!

By now, Ned had removed the gag. Nancy sprang forward to help untie the bonds that held the man's arms close to his side. Next, they cut the cords which bound his ankles together.

"I'll get some water," Nancy offered, "and see if I can find the first-aid kit."

"I think Roberto should go to a hospital," Ned told her.

"The police will be here any minute. Perhaps they'll take him," she suggested.

On the ground floor of the stable Nancy found a first-aid kit. She carried it upstairs and used an antiseptic salve on the riding master's welts. Ned gave him a dose of aromatic spirits of ammonia.

But Roberto did not regain consciousness and both were relieved when Captain McGinnis and two policemen arrived. Since Hitch was well tied up, they turned their attention to Señor Roberto.

"This man is in bad shape," the chief remarked.

"Clem," he said, addressing one of his men, "drive Señor Roberto to the hospital at once, and then return here."

The two policemen carried the riding master to their car and drove off.

Chief McGinnis now turned his attention to Hitch. The chief, with Ned's help, removed the straps from the groom and the officer began to interrogate him. Hitch insisted that he knew nothing about what had happened to Roberto. But after Chief McGinnis had shot questions and accusations at him for nearly ten minutes, Hitch finally broke down. Suddenly he screamed:

"I hate Sims' Circus and everybody in it!"

"Why?" the officer asked him.

"Circuses are evil things. Everybody who runs 'em is crazy! Now take Kroon," he said.

As Hitch mentioned the ringmaster's name, Nancy leaned forward so that she would not miss a word.

"That ringmaster—he puts up a big front, but he's the biggest thief in the world."

"How do you know?" McGinnis asked him.

Suddenly Hitch became sullen again. He said he could tell plenty about Kroon and everybody else at Sims' Circus, but why should he? What would it get him? They were the people who ought to be going to jail, not he.

Nancy heard a clock begin to strike. She counted the strokes and then cried out:

"Ned, the circus! I must get back at once or I'll be too late."

She explained that she had only twenty minutes to reach the circus, change her clothes, and appear in the finale.

The young couple dashed off. As soon as they reached

the highway, Ned gave the car full power and it sped along.

It took only a few minutes for them to reach Sims' Circus. As Nancy hopped out of Ned's car she made arrangements to meet him at the main gate later.

Erika was nervously waiting for her. She literally peeled Nancy out of her street clothes and helped her put on her riding costume. There was no time to visit the make-up artist, so the girls did a quick job of retouching Nancy's make-up.

By the time they reached the starting point for the pageant, everyone had assembled. As Nancy's group rode round for their final bow, the applause was loud and genuine. Nancy stole a quick look at her father and friends. They were clapping and waving madly.

This was the last performance in River Heights. The next day Sims' Circus would show at a town called Danford. Nancy hoped it would have as warm a reception as it had had in River Heights.

When she and Erika reached their tent, the young detective began to put on her street clothes. Erika asked why she was doing this.

"I'm going home. I'll see you in Danford tomorrow."

Erika looked worried. "It's against the rules for anyone to leave the circus overnight," she said.

"But I'm not a regular member of the troupe," Nancy replied. "I'm sure it won't make any difference if I return home for the night."

Erika advised her to speak to Dan Webster. She went to his office and fortunately found him there.

He instantly agreed with Erika. "Kroon has an insidious way of checking up on folks round here," the horse trainer told Nancy. "It would be much safer if you moved with the circus. We're leaving tonight, you know."

"Tonight?" Nancy said. "You mean we don't sleep here?"

Dan Webster laughed. He said Nancy had a lot to learn about circus life. By the time she returned home with her clothes, the tents would be down and the performers and workmen in buses and trucks on their way to Danford.

"But I'll need extra clothes," Nancy said. "How am I going to get them?"

Dan advised her to telephone her home at once and have someone bring a suitcase to her within the next fifteen minutes.

Nancy hurried from the office and went directly to the main gate where she had asked Ned Nickerson to wait for her. He was there, watching with fascination as the big top suddenly swooped to the ground.

"I see this place is packing up," he remarked, as Nancy joined him.

"And I am too," Nancy told him, quickly explaining what she had been told to do. "Ned, I'll telephone my house and have Hannah pack a suitcase. She should be home by now. Will you dash over there and bring it back to me? I'll meet you here in fifteen minutes."

"It sounds like a big order, packing any girl's suitcase in that short a time." He laughed. "But I'll be here."

Ned kept his promise and was back with the suitcase in record time. He reluctantly said goodbye to Nancy, and added that he would be very willing to drive to Danford if she needed him for further sleuthing.

Nancy waved goodbye to him and hurried back to Erika. A few moments later a truck came by and picked up their suitcases. Then the Vascon troupe hurried to board the bus which had been assigned to them.

Nancy hardly slept a wink during the trip. The ride was bumpy and the bus stuffy. At Kroon's insistence the circus group stayed together. This meant that they travelled slowly. Every once in a while one of the circus's wild animals would cry out and disturb Nancy. But the regular troupers did not seem to mind any of these disturbances and slept soundly.

The following morning at Danford, Nancy, left to herself, decided to do some detective work. She went from performer to performer asking diplomatically for information about the Kroons, the circus itself, and particularly about Lolita's parents. The young sleuth learned little that she did not already know until she came to the oldest of the clowns, a grizzled man named Leo Sanders.

He was sitting in front of his tent, looking through a scrapbook. Nancy seated herself on the ground beside him, smiled, and chattily began to question him.

"Before I divulge anything I may know," he said, "suppose you tell me why you want the information."

Quickly Nancy revealed why she was trying to help Lolita and that she suspected there might be a secret in connection with the girl's early life.

Sanders began to turn the pages of the scrapbook. Reaching a section not far from the beginning of the book, he laid it face up on Nancy's lap.

"You may find part of the answers here," he said.

· 15 ·

A Unique Admission

In the old clown's scrapbook, now on Nancy's lap, were several pictures of performers and acts of the European circus in which Lolita's parents and Sanders had appeared. Poised in flight on a double trapeze were a dainty woman and a handsome man. Under the photograph was the caption:

John and Lola Flanders.

"They were a very talented couple," the old clown remarked wistfully. "Too bad about their accident."

There were various other pictures of the famous couple, performing their difficult stunts. Nancy could see that Lolita had indeed inherited her great talent from them.

"Yes, it was unfortunate that they fell," Nancy replied. "Mr Sanders, can you tell me anything more about them?"

In answer, the man turned the page of the scrapbook. The two following pages were filled with clippings from European newspapers. None of them was in English, but the old clown helped Nancy translate them. All gave practically the same account. John Flanders had been killed outright. The injuries to his wife had been very serious and she had not been expected to live.

"But none of these clippings," said Nancy, "tell whether or not Mrs Flanders did recover."

The old clown looked around as if he feared someone might hear what he was about to tell Nancy. Finally he whispered:

"That has been a mystery all these years. One story was that Lola Flanders was taken to England and disappeared."

Nancy's pulses quickened. Probably Pietro's father *had* seen Lola Flanders in Tewkesbury!

Thinking of England reminded Nancy that she had forgotten to ask her father to start his investigation there. She decided that as soon as she finished talking with Leo Sanders, she would telephone the lawyer.

"I've heard," said Nancy to the old clown, "that John and Lola Flanders were reputed to have had a lot of money. Do you know whether this is true?"

Again Sanders spoke in a low voice. "Yes, the couple amassed a fortune with their brilliant act. Whatever became of the money no one knows. Some of the folks around here, who don't like Kroon, hint that maybe he's handling it and Lolita will never get it."

Nancy wondered about this, but Sanders had nothing further to offer. Nancy then asked the clown whether the Flanders had made all their money in the circus.

"No, not exactly," he replied. "John and Lola were very popular with nobility and other aristocrats in Europe. They were often asked to give special command performances outside the circus. They were exceedingly well paid for this."

The clown went on to say that a certain queen was

particularly fond of Lola. She had given her beautiful jewellery, including a unique bracelet.

"I only saw it once," Sanders replied, "but I never could forget it. The bracelet was solid gold and had six little horses dangling from it. Five of them represented a different gait. Two were cantering. It was the most artistic piece of jewellery I had ever seen," he concluded. "And now, I understand, you may own this very bracelet."

Nancy nodded and added, "I was told that the horse charm which Lolita wears on a necklace was given to her by her mother. Do you think it could have come from my bracelet?"

Sanders thought for a moment. He glanced at Nancy as if he were reticent to say what was in his mind. Finally he blurted out:

"I don't think the one Lolita wears is real. It doesn't glisten as much and isn't so finely made as the ones I saw on her mother's bracelet."

Here was a strange twist, the young sleuth thought. If the old clown was right, then someone had substituted an imitation horse charm for the lovely one which Lolita's mother had given her!

"I'll get my bracelet and compare the horses more closely with Lolita's," Nancy decided. She was positive that hers were the finely wrought originals.

She thanked the clown for his information. Then, before going back to her own tent, she telephoned to her father. After giving him the latest news on the case, she asked him to find out what he could in England about Lola Flanders.

After the evening performance, Nancy was wearily removing her costume before going to bed, Erika dashed in, her eyes aglow.

"Hurry and change your clothes," she said. "We're going to have a party."

Nancy sighed, admitted she was extremely tired, and thought it best if she were excused from it.

"Oh, you have to come," Erika told her. "Lolita is giving the party and she has a surprise for you!"

"A surprise for me?" Nancy repeated.

Erika would not tell her any more. The two girls changed their clothes, then her room-mate quietly led Nancy to Rancoco's trailer. Lolita and Pietro were there and several of their friends from the circus. On a table were plates of sandwiches and bottles of lemonade.

"Oh, Nancy," said Lolita, hugging her, "I'm so glad you came. I don't know where to begin to tell you all that's happened in the past few hours." Then, looking at Pietro and taking his hand, she continued, "My foster father was so cruel to me today that I can't stand another minute of it. Pietro and I are eloping!"

Nancy stared dumbfounded. Then she said, "Oh, you mustn't do that!"

A hush came over the group and Nancy realized that she had thrown a damper on the gay party.

"I don't want to seem preachy," she said. "I'd better explain what I mean."

Quickly Nancy told them that during the day she had found out several things in connection with the mystery of Lolita, her parents, and her foster parents. She felt that it would be disastrous for the aeralist to leave at this time.

"I hate to say this," Nancy went on, "but I think Lolita, and you too, Pietro, had better stay here and watch Mr Kroon."

Everyone in the trailer gasped. What did Nancy mean?

"I can't give you all the details," she said. "My father is going to help me on the case. But I'll tell you this: Lolita's own mother may still be alive. And there may be some fraud in connection with money which rightfully belongs to her or Lolita. I suspect Mr Kroon is at the back of it all."

Pietro came over to Nancy. He said it was he who had talked Lolita into eloping. It was impossible for him to stand by any longer and watch Kroon treat his foster daughter the way he was doing.

"All he's interested in is the money her performances bring," the clown said angrily. "We could easily get jobs in another circus. Nancy, you are the one to solve the mystery. We know nothing about such things. Couldn't you find out just as much about Mr Kroon if we weren't here?"

Nancy smiled. "I'm afraid," she said, "that if you two should leave, Kroon would become very suspicious. He might even blame me for your going away.

"I have a strong hunch that I may not fool him much longer. If he finds out I'm meddling in his affairs, he'll dismiss me at once. If that happens, I'll certainly need you here, Lolita, to do my sleuthing for me."

Pietro threw up his hands in a gesture of resignation. "You have convinced me, Nancy," he said. Turning to Lolita, he added, "In that case, sweetheart, I'm afraid our wedding will have to be postponed."

"I guess it *is* the wise thing to do," the dainty aerialist said. "I'd much rather have a lovely wedding and everyone who attends it to be happy."

She thanked Nancy for persuading them to wait. Then she suggested that they all eat the delicious food which Rancoco's wife had supplied, and enjoy the party anyway.

Early the next morning Nancy was surprised by a visit from her father.

"I have a lot of news for you," he told Nancy. "I thought it best not to give such confidential information to you over the telephone."

Nancy listened intently as her father revealed an interesting story. That morning the River Heights police chief, McGinnis, had called and asked Mr Drew to come down to the jail at once.

"Hitch finally made a confession," the lawyer stated. "This is the story in brief: One time while he was working with Sims' Circus, Hitch overheard Kroon accuse his wife of a kidnapping. For nearly a year the groom had blackmailed the ringmaster because of what he had heard. Then apparently Kroon would not stand for the extortion any longer, and Hitch was thrown out.

"I'm inclined to think," Mr Drew summarized, "that Kroon also had something on Hitch and this was the reason the stableman never told the story before. Well, when Hitch heard that Sims' Circus was coming to River Heights, he decided to try getting back into Kroon's good graces."

As the lawyer paused, Nancy remarked, "But he wasn't able to do it?"

Her father smiled. "This will be a surprise to you. Kroon wouldn't let Hitch back into the circus, but he did carry on an intrigue with him—against you!"

"Me?" Nancy cried.

Mr Drew nodded. He said that Hitch knew about the bracelet with the horse charms, although he had not admitted it to Nancy. Hitch had understood that it once belonged to Lolita's mother. When he found out Nancy had it, Hitch had a good talking point with Kroon.

"He told the ringmaster what he knew, and received a tidy little sum for his information. Apparently Hitch was also given the job of trying in some way to discourage you from proceeding with your work on the mystery. So he figured out that he would strangle you enough to give you a good scare!"

"But why did he harm poor Rosa?" Nancy asked.

Her father said that Hitch had done it in a fit of jealous rage. The stableman hated all equestrian performers, because he had never succeeded in becoming a good one himself.

"And what about Señor Roberto?" Nancy questioned her father.

"Hitch insists that he had nothing to do with Roberto's injuries," Mr Drew explained. "I believe he's telling the truth. But this only complicates matters. It's certain that Kroon didn't do it, since he was at the circus at the time. But it does mean that there is some unknown enemy mixed up in this whole thing. I'm inclined to think he's not a member of the circus."

"But a friend of Kroon's who is helping him cheat Lolita out of her money?" Nancy asked.

Her father smiled. "I believe you've hit the nail on the head, Nancy. And this might pertain to something else that happened in River Heights. The night that Hannah and I attended your first performance," the lawyer said, "your lovely horse-charm bracelet was stolen!"

• 16 •

A Secret Search

THE gold bracelet with the dainty little horse charms was gone!

Nancy was exceedingly upset to hear this news from her father. It had been her best clue to solving the mystery of Lolita's parents. Now she could not compare the little charms to see if the one which Lolita wore was a substitute.

Nancy told her father what the old clown, Sanders, had inferred about Lolita's trinket—that it was only an imitation.

"I strongly suspect," Nancy said, "that Kroon or Mrs Kroon may have sold the original trinket and had a cheap substitute made."

"No doubt," the lawyer agreed.

Mr Drew rose. "I must hurry back to River Heights, Nancy. I'll let you know as soon as I hear anything from England," he promised, kissing her goodbye, and left the tent.

Nancy made a point of sitting next to Lolita at supper that evening. As soon as she had an opportunity, she asked Lolita if she had mentioned to her foster parents that Nancy had the bracelet.

"Why, yes, I did. Is something the matter?"

Nancy did not reply, but asked Lolita if she could remember when she had told them.

The aerialist thought a few moments, then said it was some time during the last day that the circus was in River Heights.

There was no question in Nancy's mind that Kroon had engineered the theft. During the rest of the meal, the young sleuth kept trying to figure out how to prove her point.

"I'll bet whoever stole the bracelet brought it here to the circus," she reasoned. "And if he did, it's my guess that the bracelet is hidden in Mr Kroon's trailer."

Later, Nancy confided in Dan Webster about the theft of the bracelet and why she thought it might be in Kroon's possession. She said she was wondering how she could find out if her suspicions were correct.

"I thought perhaps I'd get in touch with the police captain," she said. "Maybe he could make a search."

Dan Webster thought that this was the sensible thing to do, but it had one big drawback.

"Kroon will know at once that you instigated the search, since it's your bracelet," he reminded Nancy. "He'll instantly make trouble for both you and the other riders in your act."

Nancy had to admit that there was merit in Dan Webster's objections. Suddenly her eyes lighted up.

"Dan," she said, "how would you like to play detective for me?"

"Me!" Dan Webster began to laugh. "You don't mean you want me to go make that search? I'd be sure to get caught."

"No, not make the search. Just lay the groundwork for me," Nancy suggested.

Dan Webster scratched his head. "Well, keep talking. I'll let you know my answer after I hear what you want me to do."

"I can't tell you now," Nancy said hurriedly. "I see Mr Kroon coming. I'll meet you in your office after the show."

The two separated, but after the show was over, Nancy returned to Webster's office. She said to the horse trainer in a low voice:

"This is what I'd like you to do. First, follow Mr Kroon until he goes to his trailer. Then call on him."

"But what excuse could I use?" Dan Webster asked.

"Oh, that's easy," Nancy said quickly. "Tell him that Rosa will not be able to perform by the end of the week. Ask him what he thinks about the new girl continuing for a while longer."

"But how is this going to find your bracelet?" the horse trainer questioned, puzzled.

"Dan," Nancy went on, "tell him that you've heard rumours of things disappearing from the circus. Watch Mr Kroon's face intently to see if there's any change of expression or if the ringmaster's eyes dart to some possible hiding place. Then tell him you've heard that one of the girls in the circus is going to ask for a police search unless something valuable which was stolen from her turns up."

As Nancy gave her instructions, Dan Webster sat gazing at the floor. He shook his head several times but did not speak. Finally he looked up.

"Miss Drew," he said, "I want to help you as much as I can. But this is a big order. I'm afraid I'd fail. You'd better count me out and get somebody else."

Nancy laughed softly. "Oh, it isn't that bad, Dan," she told him. "I'll tell you what. Suppose I stand outside the window and watch Kroon's actions. You act as innocent as you can but try to follow the lines of conversation I suggested."

At last, Dan Webster said he would try and the time was set for eleven-thirty. Nancy thanked him and hurried off to change her clothes. When Erika saw her starting out again, she asked where Nancy was going.

"To do some sleuthing. But don't be worried. I'm not going to leave the circus grounds."

Nancy hurried from the tent. Using a circuitous route to avoid as many people as possible, she went to Mr Kroon's trailer. She could hear voices inside distinctly.

No one was in sight and Nancy cautiously made her way to the side window and stood on a box. Through the window she could get a good view of the interior, but still remain out of the line of vision of those within.

Dan Webster was there, talking with Lolita's foster parents. Evidently the early part of the previously planned conversation had already taken place, because Kroon was just saying:

"The new girl's all right, but I'll let you know tomorrow about her staying with us after this week. There are certain things about her I don't like."

"What are they?" Dan asked quickly.

"Nothing that you could do anything about, Webster," the ringmaster replied. "They're personal reasons."

Dan got up, but before leaving he said, "By the way Mr Kroon, I've heard rumours about things disappearing from the circus."

Kroon gave a slight twitch and Nancy saw his eyes travel involuntarily to a bureau in the trailer. To Dan he said:

"I haven't heard anything about it. You shouldn't believe everything you hear."

"Probably not." Dan Webster gave a slightly forced

laugh. "I guess rumours fly around thick and fast in the circus."

He left the trailer and started for his own quarters. Dan had failed to carry out the last part of Nancy's instructions but it did not matter. She had found out what she wanted to know.

The bureau was probably the hiding place!

Nancy continued to eavesdrop outside the trailer, but neither Mr nor Mrs Kroon mentioned the bracelet or Dan's visit.

Presently Mrs Kroon transferred to Lolita's trailer, where she lived, apparently to watch her foster daughter's movements.

A few minutes later the window shades on both trailers were drawn and soon afterwards the lights were turned off. Nancy made her way back to her tent, convinced that her bracelet was in the bureau in Kroon's trailer. She only hoped that the ringmaster would not remove it before she had a chance to carry out the next part of her plan.

Early the following morning she went to find Lolita. She was forced to wait for several minutes while the aerialist and her foster parents finished breakfast in Mr Kroon's trailer. Finally the ringmaster left and Lolita started back to her own quarters.

Nancy beckoned her to walk to a more secluded spot where they might talk. Quickly the girl detective divulged her suspicions about the bracelet. Lolita was aghast to hear that her foster father might be a thief. Nancy said she was sorry but felt that it was necessary for Lolita to know all the facts in order to help solve the mystery.

"I want you to search that bureau," Nancy told her.

Lolita looked frightened. "But how can I?" she said.

"Mother's always in one trailer or the other."

"I'll arrange for her to leave," said Nancy. "I'll have Erika ask her to come to our tent and help with some sewing."

Lolita finally consented to the scheme. An hour later, when Mrs Kroon was safely out of the way, the aerialist went into her father's trailer. Nancy posted herself at the window. Some distance away was Dan Webster, acting as lookout.

Lolita pulled out drawer after drawer, lifting various articles aside and feeling beneath pieces of clothing. The bracelet was not in any of the drawers. Just as Lolita opened the lowest drawer, Nancy heard a low whistle. Looking up, she saw Dan Webster warning her of danger.

Rheinhold Kroon was almost at the trailer!

Through the window Nancy hissed at Lolita. The girl was so engrossed in her search that she did not hear her friend. The next moment, Kroon stepped inside. Seeing the open bureau, he thundered at Lolita:

"What are you doing?"

• 17 •

Blackout

WHEN Lolita heard someone step into the trailer, she slammed shut the bureau drawer. But her movement and the telltale clothes which trailed from the drawer gave her away completely.

"I said, what are you doing?" her foster father yelled.

He took hold of the girl's arm and yanked her round violently. As he glared at Lolita, she began to shiver with fright.

"Please don't hurt me!" she begged.

"You tell me what you were doing or I'll—" The ringmaster did not finish because of an unexpected interruption.

Fearful that Lolita's reply might give away their secret, Nancy decided upon a desperate measure. She had once learned a few ventriloquistic tricks, and now determined to use one of them. Throwing her voice to sound as if it were inside the trailer, Nancy gave an unearthly scream. Then, dashing round to the door of the trailer, she ran inside.

"I heard a scream," she said. "Lolita, is something the matter?"

Kroon glared at Nancy. The ringmaster was so taken aback that he released his hold on Lolita and said nothing for a moment.

The pretty aerialist sagged weakly on to a couch. "Oh, Nancy!" she wailed helplessly.

Kroon's eyes narrowed and Nancy felt as if they would burn right through her. The ringmaster walked towards her in menacing fashion. Nearing Nancy, he pointed a finger at her.

"Why, you little double-crosser!" he shouted.

Nancy stood her ground, not moving an inch. Out of the corner of her eye she could see Dan Webster in the doorway. Should she need any protection, it was near at hand.

"Nancy, eh?" Kroon yelled. "You're Nancy Drew, that self-styled detective, and you sneaked in here to spy on the circus!"

Still Nancy said nothing. This seemed to infuriate the man. Towering above her, his face so red that Nancy thought he might have a stroke, he continued to wave a finger in her face.

"I knew you'd joined the circus and I let you stay because you were a good rider," he went on. "But I've had spies trailing you. So don't think you've put anything over on me, you little sneak! You get out of this circus now and stay out!"

"But what will happen to the Vascons' act?" Lolita spoke up.

Kroon said that Rosa would perform that afternoon or the whole troupe could leave the circus at once. In no case was Nancy Drew to appear. She was to pack her things immediately and go back to River Heights.

In the doorway Dan Webster could remain silent no longer. Stepping inside, he began to plead for Nancy to remain. The ringmaster would not listen.

Nancy, seeing that it was useless to argue with him, looked straight at Kroon and said, "I'll go, but not until you give me back my bracelet!"

Kroon gave a slight start, but instantly recovered his poise.

"What are you talking about?" he bellowed.

"I'm talking about a gold bracelet with horse charms. The bracelet was stolen from my house and I have good reason to believe that you have it."

Kroon's eyes blazed. He said that he ought to have Nancy arrested for accusing him of being a thief. It was defamation of character. It was only because of her age that he would not prosecute.

"Now get out of here, every one of you!" he yelled and shoved them all through the doorway.

He followed the others outside, then slammed the door and locked it.

"Lolita," he said, "go to your quarters. And if you ever dare to communicate with Nancy Drew again, I'll punish you in a way you'll never forget."

He turned towards Nancy and said sneeringly, "I suppose I ought to thank you for helping us out in the circus. But, under the circumstances, you don't deserve anything. Goodbye and good riddance!"

The ringmaster strode away. Lolita, ill from fright, hurried off to her own trailer. Nancy felt it best not to intrude.

She walked off with Dan Webster, who asked her if she were willing to take a chance on remaining with the circus. Surprised, the young sleuth remarked that this would hardly be safe.

"I would hate to see the Vascons fired," Dan said. "But I'm afraid that's what will happen. I dropped into the doctor's this morning. He said Rosa would not be able to ride for at least a month.'

"Oh," said Nancy, "you wouldn't expect me to hide in the circus and substitute for her all that time?"

Dan Webster shook his head, saying he could not expect that much. But the following week, the circus did not have commitments for a few days.

"During that time I'm sure we can find another substitute rider," Dan told her.

"In other words," said Nancy, "you want me to finish out this week."

"That's the idea. How about it?"

Nancy said she was willing, if she could possibly get away with the subterfuge. It would give her a chance to do more sleuthing in the circus. On the spur of the moment, a plan came to her.

"Suppose I room with someone else in the circus," she said. "Rosa can move back to Erika's tent. Since Mr Kroon probably will be watching to see that she goes into the big top, Rosa might dress and ride in the parade. Then, when it's time for her act, I'll substitute for her."

Dan Webster smiled. "We'll do it! I'll arrange for you to stay at the hospital tent. Kroon would never think of looking for you there." He winked. "And besides, the doc and his nurse are good friends of mine."

Nancy now told the horse trainer that she was fearful Kroon might return to his trailer and take the bracelet away. She did not want this to happen and asked if Dan Webster could possibly play detective for her again.

The horse trainer laughed and said that he did not believe he could get away with it a second time. Kroon would be sure to know something was up. Dan suggested that one of his midget friends act as lookout.

"Little Will is to be trusted implicitly," he said.

Nancy knew the pleasant little man and consented to the plan. Then Nancy told Dan Webster that she was going to telephone her friends, Bess and George, in River Heights and ask them to drive over to Danford.

"Kroon may discover the ruse we've planned," she said. "In that case, I'll need some transportation home. And besides, the girls can relieve Little Will in watching Mr Kroon's trailer."

At once Nancy telephoned George, who promised that she and Bess would start immediately for Danford.

"I'll be hiding in the hospital tent, George. Come there."

It was shortly before the afternoon performance that the cousins arrived. Bess was aghast to hear what had transpired and tried her best to coax Nancy into going home with her and George at once. But the girl detective contended that it was important for her to stay.

Just before time for the parade, Dan Webster came to tell Nancy that Little Will was hard at work. He had watched the trailer constantly. Mrs Kroon had entered it directly after luncheon and had not come out since.

"How would it be if I relieve your midget friend now?" George proposed. "I don't care about seeing the circus performance again."

Nancy thought that this was a good idea. George went off, but Bess remained with Nancy. She would act as messenger to carry the riding costume back and forth. Presently the gong sounded for the parade to begin.

Rosa, seated on the beautiful horse, took her position, and Nancy watched from a nearby place of concealment. As the girl detective had predicted, Kroon was on hand to meet her. He smiled in satisfaction.

Apparently completely satisfied that his orders were being carried out, the ringmaster did not stay in the tent when the Vascon troupe entered. Nancy felt a little nervous at first but did her act well.

When the performance was over, she quickly ran to the hospital tent. After she removed her costume, Bess hurried with it to Rosa. She returned in a few minutes and reported that her cousin was still on duty. Little Will had said he would eat his supper and then take George's place until he had to perform again.

"Nancy, you can't keep up this watching and performing. You'll need sleep," Bess said worriedly. "George and I can't help you much longer. We'll have to go home in a little while."

"Oh, please stay overnight," Nancy requested. "By tomorrow I'm sure we'll find out about the bracelet.

Would you mind calling home and telling your mother and George's you'll be here?"

Bess finally agreed and made the call. Then, fearfully, she went off to take George's place while her cousin came to eat her supper in the hospital tent.

The evening performance came to a close, without the ringmaster suspecting that Nancy had been substituting for Rosa. Relieved, Nancy had just reached the hospital tent when George rushed in.

"Nancy! News!" she cried.

She related how Kroon had sneaked up to the trailer from the rear. Mrs Kroon had handed him a small package through the side window. The ringmaster, in turn, had given it to the son of one of the aerial artists and told him to mail it.

"I followed the boy downtown towards the post office," said George. "As we got near a crossing, I started to run and pretended to bump into him. He dropped the package and I looked at the address on it. And listen to this: it was going to Lola Flanders, care of Tristam Booking Agency in New York City!"

"Oh, George, you're wonderful!" Nancy cried gleefully. "We'll go right to the telephone, call up the local police chief, and ask him to get in touch with the New York police. They'll be able to investigate that package and the booking agency too, and even find Mrs Flanders!"

The excited girls raced from the tent and hurried to the telephone booth. George waited outside, while Nancy stepped in and closed the door. She picked up the receiver and put in a coin. When there was no response, Nancy realized that the telephone was out of order.

"I'll ask George to run down to headquarters and

take my message to the chief," she decided.

Opening the door, Nancy was amazed to find that her friend was gone. As she looked round, suddenly a thick dark cloth was drawn over her head—tighter and tighter.

Nancy struggled, but it was useless. She finally blacked out!

• 18 •

George's Discovery

NANCY became conscious of the rumble and harsh clatter of wheels. At first it seemed far away, then grew louder and louder.

Slowly she opened her eyes but could see nothing. Her brain was foggy and she had no idea where she was. As her mind cleared, Nancy realized she was bound and gagged.

"Oh, yes," she recalled. "When I came out of that telephone booth, someone put a cloth over my head and I blacked out."

Nancy now realized that she was in a moving vehicle. The steady rhythm of the wheels told her that she was in a train. Was it a sleeping compartment?

"Probably not," Nancy decided. "I'm lying on the floor. I must be in a freight car."

As her strength returned, she tried to get out of her bonds, but her struggles were futile. Whoever had tied the knots had done a good job.

"Oh, if I could only remove this gag!" she thought.

She tried rubbing her cheek against the floor to accomplish it, but again her efforts were unsuccessful. There was not a sound within the car and Nancy decided that she was alone. As she wondered where the freight train was going and how long a trip it might be, someone not far away from her gave a great sigh. Nancy shuddered. Was this person a guard?

Once more she endeavoured to loosen the ropes which bound her arms and legs. She managed to slide them an inch, but they still remained tightly round her.

As Nancy got over her fright, it occurred to her that the other person in the car might be a prisoner as well. George had disappeared rather mysteriously. Could she be the person who had sighed?

Nancy wriggled herself in the direction from which the sound had come. Finding the other person's hand, she squirmed. It was cold and unresponsive. But upon investigation, she was convinced of one thing: it was a girl's hand.

Inching herself upward, Nancy's hand came to a rope. The other person was bound as well as herself!

Moving still farther along the floor, Nancy felt the girl's face. There was a gag over it, but by twisting and turning, Nancy managed, after some difficulty, to loosen the knot and remove the gag.

Nancy ran her fingers over the girl's features and came to the conclusion that she was indeed George Fayne. She mumbled as loudly as she could:

"George! George! Wake up!"

Presently the girl stirred and Nancy's heart leaped in

relief. After muttering some unintelligible words, George finally said:

"Where am I?"

The girl detective replied that they were in a freight car. Where the train was going, she had no idea—it might be heading for the coast.

"But we're going to get out of here," she said with determination.

"You must have a gag over your mouth," said George. "Your voice sounds so different."

"I have," said Nancy. "See if you can get it off." She turned her head away from George, and after several futile attempts, George finally managed to loosen it.

"That's better. Thanks a lot," Nancy said. "Now I'll unfasten your ropes."

George turned on her side and Nancy felt for the knots. Untying them was slow work. Her hands ached from the effort.

George, freed, suggested that she untie Nancy's hands before freeing her own legs. She felt for the knots. Upon finding the first one, she began the difficult task of loosening it.

But she persevered and at last was rewarded. There were two other ropes bound around Nancy's arms, and it was a good twenty minutes before George was able to get them off.

"Oh, that feels wonderful!" Nancy said. "Now to get these ropes off our legs."

The process took a long time, and while the girls were at it, they began to discuss what had happened to them.

"I guess I'm responsible for all this," said George. "That boy who took the package to the post office possibly told Mr Kroon what happened the minute he got back to the circus."

Nancy agreed and added, "He wanted to make sure that we didn't communicate with the police before he had a chance to retrieve the package."

"You mean he'll try to get it from the post office?"

Nancy said that she did not think the ringmaster would dare attempt this. But he probably had planned to keep George and Nancy prisoners until the package could reach New York and be delivered.

"But here's where my work to stop him begins," she said resolutely. "Here goes the last knot."

Within a few minutes George also was free.

The girls made their way to the side of the car. The door was easy to find, and the mechanism which opened it. But try as they might, they could not budge the door an inch.

"It's probably locked from the outside," Nancy decided.

Suddenly George had an idea. "Maybe there's a hatch in the roof of this car," she said.

"I don't think so," Nancy answered. "Only refrigerator cars have them. But I'll be glad to find out. Do you think you can hold me on your shoulders while I investigate the roof?"

George leaned over and Nancy climbed to her shoulders. But trying to stand up straight and balance herself in the swaying car was even more difficult than standing on a cantering horse.

At last Nancy was able to stand on George's shoulders and reach up to the roof of the car. After feeling around for several minutes, Nancy came to the conclusion that there was no hatch. She jumped down.

"George," she said, "we never thought of a door on the other side of this car."

Annoyed at themselves, they hurried to find out.

Their fingers found a latch! The girls hardly dared hope the door would be unlocked, but as they pulled on it, the sliding panel moved!

"Thank goodness!" George cried. "Now we can get out of this prison."

"Not yet," Nancy told her, as she saw the scenery flashing past them. "We're travelling about fifty miles an hour."

She guessed at the time. It must be an hour or so after dawn.

"Where do you suppose we are?" George asked.

On every side stretched cultivated fields, but there was not a house in sight.

"I wonder what the chances are of the freight slowing down," said Nancy.

As if in answer to her wish, the train reached a long gradient and began to lose speed. In a short time it was moving very slowly.

A few minutes later the freight train slowed down to about five miles an hour. The two girls selected a favourable spot and jumped from the slowly moving train. They were free!

Nancy and George started rapidly across a field before anyone in the freight train might become aware of their presence. A quarter of a mile farther on, the girls came to a road.

"Oh, hallelujah, there's a farmhouse!" George cried. "I never was so glad to see a house in my life!"

Nancy grinned. She was pretty delighted about it herself. At the farmhouse they found an elderly couple. They looked searchingly at the dishevelled girls when Nancy asked to use their telephone.

"I guess so," the man answered. "Where you two be comin' from this early hour of the mornin'?"

"Why—uh—we were out for a drive," Nancy replied haltingly. "We—uh—left our car over by the railroad."

"Broke down, eh?" the man said, as he led the girl to the telephone.

Nancy put in a call to her home, reversing the charges. It hardly seemed as if the telephone had started ringing when Hannah answered. The frantic woman wanted to know if Nancy was all right.

"I'm fine, Hannah," she said. "Don't worry about me. I'll be home after a while."

"Where are you?" the housekeeper asked.

"Just a minute. I'll find out."

Nancy turned to the man and asked where she was. He said not far from the town of Black River. The girl relayed this to Hannah.

"My goodness," she said, "that's about a hundred miles from here."

Nancy said that if she needed any assistance in getting home she would call again. She asked the housekeeper to notify George's parents that their daughter was with her and was all right.

After Nancy had completed the telephone call, she asked the farmer if it would be possible for him to drive the girls to town.

"I'll be glad to," he said. "I was going anyway, soon as I have my breakfast. Have you girls eaten yet?"

When they told him no, his wife invited the girls to join them.

During the meal, the kindly couple were curious to learn more about their visitors, but the girls were wary of saying anything.

Upon arriving in Black River, the girls immediately went to the State Police office, and after giving their names, told them what had happened.

"We haven't a shred of evidence to prove who was responsible," said Nancy, "only suspicions. And the police are already working on the case, so I'm not asking your help except to get as home. We haven't a penny with us."

"I can do that," the officer said, smiling. He took some money from a drawer and handed it to Nancy. "Return the cash when it's convenient."

The girls thanked him and went to the station. A short time later they boarded a train to River Heights and at nine o'clock reached home.

Mr Drew hugged his daughter, and Hannah wiped away tears of joy. After the greetings and explanations were over, Nancy said ruefully:

"I won't dare go back to Sims' Circus, I suppose. I wonder what will happen to the Vascons' act."

"That's no longer your worry, Nancy," her father said firmly. "What's more, you're leaving town at once. Let Kroon think his diabolical plan was a success."

"Where am I going?" Nancy asked.

"How would you like to visit Aunt Eloise and continue to work on the case in New York?" he suggested.

Nancy kissed her father. "Dad, you're a genius. I can't think of anything I'd rather do!"

19

New York Yields a Lead

As Nancy quickly packed her bags in order to catch the afternoon plane to New York, she discussed further angles of the case with her father.

"Don't you think George ought to go away, too," she asked.

"I think it would be a very good idea," her father replied. "Why don't you take her with you?"

Nancy telephoned her friend and learned that the Fayne family already had planned for George to be out of town for a while. They were taking her on a motor trip.

Nancy's next call was to Bess. It had been she who had learned of the disappearance of Nancy and George from the circus. Bess had summoned Mr Drew, who had gone at once to question Kroon. The ringmaster had told the lawyer he had discharged Nancy because she was not a regular member of the circus. He had assumed that Nancy, of course, had gone home.

Mr Drew drove his daughter to the airport and waved goodbye as she boarded the plane. Nancy settled herself comfortably and soon fell asleep from exhaustion. By the time she reached New York, Nancy was refreshed and ready to continue work on the case.

Her father had given her a letter of introduction from Police Chief McGinnis in River Heights to Captain Smith of the New York Police Department, who had been assigned to the Tristam Booking Agency investigation.

Nancy toyed with the idea of going at once to call on the police captain. But she knew her aunt would be waiting, since Nancy's father had said he was telephoning to her from the airport. Nancy took a taxi to Eloise Drew's apartment and soon the two were embracing each other.

While they ate supper, the conversation turned to the mystery. Aunt Eloise begged her niece to be careful and not undertake any sleuthing alone. Nancy promised.

"First thing tomorrow morning I'm going down to talk to Police Captain Smith," she said. "I wonder what he found out about Lola Flanders. Wouldn't it be wonderful if she really were Lolita's mother?"

Aunt Eloise was not so sure of this. Perhaps the woman had changed a great deal during a period of ten years. It seemed very strange that she had not been in touch with her daughter.

"At least Lolita knows nothing about this," Nancy replied. "If it seems best not to tell her about Lola, I shall keep it a secret."

The situation bothered Nancy. She tossed restlessly in bed for nearly an hour after turning out the light. But finally she dropped off to sleep. Directly after breakfast, however, she set off for Captain Smith's headquarters.

She presented the letter of introduction to the sergeant on duty and he took it to the captain. In a moment the sergeant returned, inviting Nancy to follow him. He showed her into the office, then closed the door and left.

"I'm glad to meet you, Miss Drew," the officer said, smiling. "Chief McGinnis and I were buddies in the Army some years ago. He tells me that you're quite a detective."

Nancy blushed slightly and admitted that she had solved some cases. Then she turned the conversation from herself and asked:

"Have you found Lola Flanders?"

"We don't know yet," Captain Smith told her. "We're still checking."

He went on to say that one of their detectives had called at the Tristam Booking Agency. He had been able to learn little from either the owner or his secretary.

"They're cagey people," the officer said. "They told our detective that they never discuss their clients' private affairs."

"But you did find out something about Lola Flanders?" Nancy asked.

"Yes. She's a young dancer and uses the stage name of Millie Francine."

"A young dancer!" Nancy repeated. "Then this Lola Flanders is not the person I'm looking for."

Nancy sat lost in thought for a few moments. This was a turn of events she had not expected. Who was this young Lola Flanders? Was she a relative of Lolita's, perhaps?

"Where is the dancer now?" Nancy asked the police captain.

"She's working on the West Coast," he replied. "I've made a check. The story is correct—as far as it goes."

The captain said that the police were watching the mails. The suspected package from Danford had not arrived yet. As soon as it did, it would be impounded and X-rayed.

Nancy said that she was staying with her aunt and gave Miss Drew's address. The police captain said that he would call as soon as the package had been examined. She returned to the apartment and waited for the call.

Just before noon, Captain Smith telephoned.

"The package is here," he told her. "Can you come right over to headquarters?"

"Indeed I can," said Nancy. "I'll be there in a jiffy."

When she reached Captain Smith's headquarters, he pointed to a bracelet lying on his desk.

"Is that yours?" he asked.

At first glance Nancy thought that it was, but when she picked it up, she changed her mind. Although it was very similar to hers, this bracelet had six horses on it. Furthermore, the bracelet was much darker in colour and looked older.

"I'm afraid this isn't mine," Nancy said, considerably embarrassed. She told him why.

Captain Smith took the bracelet from her. He walked to a window and looked at it in the strong light.

"I'm no expert at judging jewellery," he said, "but I'd say this bracelet might have been tampered with to change its appearance."

Nancy hurried to the window and examined the bracelet more closely herself. "It does look as if this one horse had been attached recently. It's in the place where the charm on my bracelet was missing."

Captain Smith said that it was a trick among jewel thieves to change the appearance of jewellery by darkening or lighting the colour of it. It was his guess that this had been done to the bracelet.

"May I use your telephone and call Chief McGinnis?" Nancy asked him. "I'd like him to check with the girl at the circus who has a necklace with a horse charm on it similar to these."

"Go ahead," the captain said.

He left Nancy and she put in a call to River Heights. After talking with Nancy a few minutes, Chief McGinnis promised to get in touch with the police in the town where the circus was now staying.

"I'll call Captain Smith as soon as I have the answer," he said.

Nancy was sure that the reply would not come for several hours, so she went home to have luncheon with her aunt. They had just finished eating when the telephone rang. Captain Smith was reporting that Lolita still had her horse-charm necklace.

"Captain Smith," Nancy said, "will you go with me and my aunt to the shop where she purchased the bracelet? I'm sure that the owner will be able to identify the one you're holding if it is the original."

The officer said he would be glad to accompany them. He made arrangements to meet Nancy and her aunt in twenty minutes.

At the appointed time the three walked into the shop. After hearing their story, Mr Abrams, the shop owner, made a quick examination of the bracelet and confirmed the captain's theory that it had been tampered with recently.

Using a special powder and a piece of chamois, he began to rub the bracelet. Presently the stain which had been used on it began to rub off. In a few minutes the bracelet looked exactly as Nancy remembered it except for the addition of the sixth horse.

"Whoever put this one charm on," said Mr Abrams "was an amateur. This was a hurried, clumsy job."

Nancy's thoughts flew at once to Mr and Mrs Kroon

Had the woman attached it and wrapped the bracelet for mailing while George and Little Will had been acting as lookouts at the trailer? Had the Kroons stolen the original charm from Lolita's necklace some time ago and kept it, hoping to locate the valuable bracelet and attach the missing horse, and sell the jewellery at a high price?

"Mr Abrams," said Nancy, "would you mind looking in your records and telling me where you purchased the bracelet?"

"I'd be very glad to," the shop owner said, smiling.

He disappeared into a back room and was gone for some time. Finally he returned and handed Nancy a piece of paper.

"I purchased the bracelet from a London pawnshop," he said. "Here's the name and address."

Nancy and the others thanked Mr Abrams for his information and left the shop. When they reached the sidewalk, Captain Smith gave Nancy the bracelet. She thanked him and asked the captain if he would cable the shop in London and find out who had signed the pawn ticket.

"Certainly," Captain Smith said, "only I believe I'll do it through the London police. But it will take hours."

The following morning Nancy waited impatiently for a call from Captain Smith. He telephoned her about eleven o'clock.

"It begins to look as though you were getting somewhere in your mystery, Miss Drew," he said. "The pawn ticket was signed with a nervous scrawl which was hardly legible. The pawnshop owner thought it looked something like Laura Flynn."

"Oh, it could have been Lola Flanders!" Nancy cried excitedly.

"I believe you're right," the captain agreed. "The ticket was signed three years ago. The shop keeps things for only two years. That's why they were able to sell it."

After putting down the telephone receiver, Nancy continued to think about this latest news. Suddenly her eyes sparkled. She picked up the telephone and dialled long-distance. Nancy gave the operator the number of her father's office. When he answered, she told him what she had discovered since her arrival in New York. Then suddenly she said:

"Dad, will you fly to London with me right away?"

· 20 ·

A Vicious Trick

THERE was an exclamation of surprise on the other end of the telephone as Mr Drew asked Nancy if he had heard her correctly.

"Did you say 'Let's fly to London?' "

"That's right, Dad. How about it? You need a vacation, anyhow, and you can help me solve the mystery. Who knows, we may find Lolita's mother and bring her back with us."

Nancy could hear her father mumbling. Here and there she caught a word which she recognized as the names of various clients. Presently Mr Drew said:

"All right, Nancy. We'll go. I have some important things pending, but they can wait a week or so. Suppose you see if you can get reservations for tomorrow."

Nancy said she would call him back as soon as she found out.

"In the meantime, Dad, will you please try to find out if there have been any new developments in Sims' Circus?"

"I can answer part of your query right now," her father replied. "Bess called here a little while ago. She said that Lolita had been in touch with her. The poor girl is very unhappy. Kroon is keeping her virtually a prisoner. What's worse, he has dismissed Pietro."

"That is bad news," Nancy remarked. "Where is Pietro?"

Mr Drew said that he did not know. Kroon did not permit Lolita to receive mail or telephone calls of any kind. She had made the call to Bess through Erika.

"Lolita is hoping that Pietro will get in touch with Bess, and that Bess will be able to forward the message to Erika."

Since this was all the information the lawyer could give Nancy at the moment, they said goodbye. Nancy at once got in touch with the airport to find out about reservations. She was told that there were no seats available, but that she would be notified should any cancellations come in.

Nancy waited impatiently. Finally she decided to phone her father to tell him that it would not be necessary for him to take the evening plane from River Heights.

"When is the next one you could get?" his daughter asked.

Mr Drew said that one left at two in the morning. It

would arrive in New York in plenty of time to catch the afternoon overseas plane.

"Call me again if you have any luck with reservations," he directed her. "By the way, I have more news for you. The police interviewed Kroon about the package to Lola Flanders. The man insisted that he never had anything to do with sending a package to a Lola Flanders and knew no one by that name."

"But what about the boy who mailed the package for him?" Nancy questioned.

"Oh, he's exonerated," Mr Drew replied. "The boy says he mailed a package for Mr Kroon, all right, but he didn't read the name and address on it."

As she put down the receiver, Nancy wondered whether the boy had been coached by Kroon to say that he had not looked at the address. Three hours later the telephone rang. Nancy hurried to it and was delighted to learn that the call was from the airport.

"I have your two reservations, Miss Drew," the young woman at the other end of the wire informed her.

Nancy immediately telephoned her father and told him the good news. He said he was glad to hear it because he had been looking forward to a vacation with his daughter.

"Ned is coming with me to see us off," Mr Drew added.

Nancy smiled as she hung up. It would be nice having a little send-off party with Ned and Aunt Eloise at the airport.

She and her aunt rose early in order to meet the plane from River Heights. To her amazement, not only did her father and Ned step off the airliner, but Pietro as well.

"Oh, it's good to see you, Pietro!" Nancy cried.

Ned looked as if he did not wholly approve of Nancy's extremely friendly greeting to the clown. And a frown creased his forehead when Pietro announced that he was going to London with the Drews to see his father.

After Pietro had been introduced to Aunt Eloise, the group found a taxi and drove to Miss Drew's apartment.

As soon as luncheon was over, Nancy said that she wanted to telephone Captain Smith and find out what more had been learned about the Tristam Booking Agency.

"I think we have a rather important clue," the officer told her. "Our men have been watching the mail which has been arriving for Lola Flanders. She has been receiving dividend cheques in rather large amounts."

The captain went on to say that it seemed very strange for a young dancer of Lola Flanders' apparent wealth to be tied up with a second-rate booking agency. And furthermore, why would she have this kind of mail sent to the agency, anyway?

Nancy had formed her own conclusions on this matter. It seemed to her proof that Reinhold Kroon was using the agency as a cover-up. He was stealing money which belonged to the real Lola Flanders and using Millie Francine as a front.

As Nancy discussed the latest findings with her father, she remarked, "Do you suppose Millie Francine is innocent and that Kroon and Tristam have given her the name Lola Flanders to make their underhanded schemes seem legitimate?"

Mr Drew said this was very likely. He hoped that by the time he and his daughter returned from England the police would have found the answer to her question. He looked at his watch.

"We'd better leave now," he told the others.

On the way to the airport, Nancy's heart began to beat a little faster. She was off on another exciting adventure!

The Drews and Pietro checked in. Each had a large suitcase for the baggage compartment and an overnight case to carry. While waiting for the moment when she might board the plane, Nancy and her friends walked outside.

At this moment a trans-Atlantic jet swooped in. It was the largest one any of them had ever seen and they watched it in fascination as the pilot landed the great ship.

"My, she's a beauty!" Ned exclaimed admiringly.

Nancy was so intent that for a moment she did not notice a strange man who had joined the group. Then, suddenly, out of the corner of her eye, she realized he had picked up her overnight bag and was running off with it. Without waiting to tell the others what had happened, she ran after the thief.

"Stop!" she called to him.

He went on and now was holding the case in front of him. As Nancy lessened the distance between herself and the fleeing man, she thought he was trying to open the bag which was not locked. Why? Surely there was nothing in it worth removing.

"Stop!" Nancy shouted again.

Bystanders, thinking she was merely trying to attract the man's attention did not interfere, so finally Nancy cried:

"Stop, thief!"

This time the command was heeded. The man dropped the bag and fled. Nancy picked it up and started to follow the thief but decided it probably would be a long chase and she might miss the plane.

Noticing that a corner of her pink-flowered robe was protruding from the bag, Nancy was sure the man had opened it. She must find out what he was up to!

Nancy hurried into a women's lounge and sat down in a chair. As the attendant looked on, Nancy put the overnight case on her lap and opened it wide.

Acrid fumes rose from among the disarrayed clothes and toilet articles. An open bottle lay in their midst. Before Nancy could close down the lid, she began to cough and choke. The next moment, the acid affected her eyes.

"I can't see!" Nancy groaned in alarm.

• 21 •

A Lucky Hunch

At Nancy's outcry, the attendant rushed forward. "What's the trouble, miss?" she asked.

"My eyes!" Nancy repeated. "Someone put acid in my bag. Oh, please do something!"

The frightened attendant said she would take Nancy to the first-aid station. Guiding the stricken girl through the waiting-room with one hand and carrying her bag in the other, the woman led Nancy to the airport's infirmary. A nurse hurried forward to take charge.

Nancy quickly explained what had happened, and at once she and her bag were taken into the doctor's office.

The odour of the fumes was very evident and the physician recognized them at once. He took down a bottle of oily fluid and gauze sponges from a shelf. Soaking a sponge, he dabbed it on her eyes.

"Take that bag out in the fresh air!" he ordered.

The nurse hurriedly went off with it. The physician continued to work on Nancy. Presently she was able to see but only dimly.

"Will my sight be permanently impaired?" she asked fearfully.

"No, fortunately. If you had spilled the acid in your eyes, you could have been blinded. But the fumes merely affected them momentarily."

The soothing medication did its work well, and in a few minutes Nancy was able to see distinctly again. She thanked the physician for his quick help.

"I'm glad I was handy," he said, smiling. Then he sobered. "Would you mind telling me why you were carrying that deadly acid with you?"

Nancy told as much of the story as she felt was advisable. The physician's eyebrows raised in amazement.

"So you're a girl detective?" he said admiringly. "The man who tried to harm you ought to be jailed for malicious intent."

Outside, Mr Drew and his companions wondered what had happened to Nancy. She had disappeared so suddenly while they were looking at the incoming plane that they had not noticed where she had gone.

"She probably went to telephone again," Ned said.

"Well, I wish she'd get back," Mr Drew remarked. "We'll be taking off in a few minutes."

Ned had been staring at a rather unusual sight a short distance away. A woman's overnight bag lay wide open, and a white uniformed nurse and a policeman were examining its contents.

Ned laughed and pointed out the scene to Miss Drew. "That has all the earmarks of a mystery," he said. "Nancy ought to be here to solve it."

But Aunt Eloise did not smile. She had recognized the pink-flowered dressing robe which she knew belonged to Nancy, and told the others.

"What could have happened?" Miss Drew said, worried.

The whole group hurried over to the policeman and inquired what the trouble was. He replied in an impatient tone of voice, "Oh, some fool girl was carrying a bottle of deadly acid in her bag. It got uncorked somehow. A doc in the first-aid station is taking care of her."

"What!" Mr Drew cried. Turning to the nurse, he said he was the girl's father. "Please take us to her at once."

Reaching the infirmary, they burst into the doctor's office.

"Nancy! What happened?" Mr Drew cried.

Quickly his daughter gave him the correct details.

The doctor declared that Nancy was all right to travel, so she hurried outside with the others. She could give the policeman only a hazy description of the man who had tampered with her bag, because she had seen little more than his back.

Nancy stooped to the ground and looked in dismay at her suitcase. The acid had spilled on some of the articles and the robe was ruined. Luckily, it had not damaged the bag itself, and Nancy was able to retrieve some of her belongings.

Over the loud-speaker came the announcement:

"Flight 1205. Passengers for Flight 1205 aboard!"

Mr Drew turned to his daughter. "Nancy, are you sure you feel well enough to make the trip?"

"I'm perfectly all right, really I am," she replied.

Pietro and the Drews said goodbye and found their seats in the plane. A few minutes later the door was closed. The pilot taxied down the runway, then waited for clearance. Finally the overseas airliner roared along the ground and took off gracefully.

Nancy watched from the window as long as land was in sight. Then, as the plane went higher and higher into the clouds, she settled down to read the magazine Aunt Eloise had given her. But reading seemed to hurt her eyes and she decided not to take a chance of straining them. When evening came, Mr Drew changed seats with Pietro. Nancy asked the clown how long it was since he had seen his father.

"Several years," Pietro answered. "Not since Dad retired. You'll like him," the young man went on. "My father is one of the kindest and most humorous men I have ever known."

The three discussed the history of the circus at great length—in fact, until Mr Drew invited them to take a meal with him. They had dinner and then decided to have a long night's sleep.

When they landed, Nancy and her companions were among the first to leave the plane. After going through the customs, they walked towards the exit gate. Pietro looked eagerly for his father. Suddenly he saw him and started to run.

Nancy enjoyed watching the joyful reunion as the two men clasped each other in their arms. When the Drews walked up, Pietro introduced his father.

"This is the young lady I wrote you about," the

clown said, "the one who is trying to straighten out everything so that Lolita and I can be married."

"Then I am doubly glad to meet you, Miss Drew," the older man said, smiling. He shook her hand warmly.

They took a taxi and soon were riding through the busy streets of the city.

Pietro told his father what had happened to Nancy just before they took off. A frightened look came over the older man's face and he remarked that he hoped Nancy would be perfectly safe in England.

"Oh, I'll be all right," Nancy insisted. "But you men will have to be patient with me while I do some shopping. That awful man and his acid ruined some rather vital parts of my wardrobe."

After breakfast, the group set off for the shopping trip and a visit to the pawnshop from which Nancy's bracelet had come. When they reached the door of a large department store, Mr Drew suggested that Nancy be given half an hour for her shopping.

"We men will look around and meet you here," he suggested, as he handed her some English money.

Hurrying from one counter to another, Nancy not only bought the necessary articles for which she had come but several others as well.

"And I ought to pick up a few souvenirs while I'm here," she told herself. "I must get something for Hannah. And George and Bess, too. They were certainly wonderful, helping me on the mystery."

Nancy actually forgot the time, and when she rejoined her companions, was profuse in her apology for having kept them waiting twenty minutes.

The pawnshop was not far away. The owner proved to be very helpful. Though it had been three years since the woman who had signed her name as Laura

Flynn had visited his shop, he remembered her well.

"I felt so sorry for her," he said. "She seemed frightened and ill at ease. Apparently it was very hard for her to decide to part with the bracelet." When he described her, Nancy was at once reminded of Lolita. Apparently mother and daughter strongly resembled each other.

"She's the one I saw in Tewkesbury, all right!" Mr Pietro cried.

Nancy wanted to set off at once to look for Lola Flanders. But the others insisted that she should do some sight-seeing in London. And Mr Drew wanted to call on the lawyer with whom he had communicated. The following morning they set off, however.

Mr Drew had hired a comfortable car to use during their stay in England. Since it would be a little confusing at first to drive on the left side of the road, Pietro's father offered to take the wheel.

Nancy was charmed with the countryside as they came nearer and nearer to the town of Tewkesbury. Presently Mr Pietro asked her where she intended to search. He had already made inquiries in every place he could think of.

"I have an idea that Lola Flanders may be in some nursing home," said Nancy.

"That's a good hunch," her father remarked. "Mr Pietro, how can we go about finding out where the nursing homes are?"

The retired clown suggested that they go to the medical registry. He was sure they could find out there. He drove to the building and went inside with Nancy. They learned that there were two large and eight small nursing homes in the area.

As they went from one to another, Nancy asked if

they had a patient by either the name of Lola Flanders or Laura Flynn. After they had inquired at six of them and received a negative reply, everyone in the group except Nancy became discouraged.

"Why, we have four more to investigate," she said cheerfully.

The last home they came to was a very shabby place. The house was in disrepair and in need of painting. Unlike others in the neighbourhood, it had a weedy, run-down garden.

The woman who answered Nancy's knock proved to be the owner of the home. Her name was Mrs Ayres and she was as shabby looking as her place. But in a moment, Nancy forgot all this. One of her patients was named Lola Flanders!

"I've come all the way from the United States to see her," said Nancy excitedly.

Mrs Ayres stared at the visitor. "Well, it's too bad you went to all that trouble, miss," she said. "You can't see Lola Flanders. She's a victim of amnesia!"

· 22 ·

The Hunt Narrows

Mrs Ayres started to close the door of her nursing home.

"Oh, please!" Nancy said hurriedly. "I must talk to you."

The woman rather grudgingly invited Nancy to step inside and ushered her into a dark living-room whose furnishings were threadbare and dilapidated.

"Would you mind telling me something about Mrs Flanders?" Nancy asked, smiling disarmingly. "If she is the person I'm looking for, I know her daughter well. She would like very much to get in touch with her mother."

Mrs Ayres hesitated a few moments, apparently wanting to be sure that it was safe to talk freely to the stranger. Finally she said:

"Lola Flanders is an American. She worked in a circus. But she had a bad fall. I don't know much about that part of it. First I knew, a man named Jones came here and asked me if I could board Lola. After a while he brought her. That's all there is to the story."

Nancy did not think so. Several questions popped into her mind.

"How long ago was that?"

"Let me see," Mrs Ayres said. "It was nearly ten years ago."

The date exactly fitted the time when Lolita had been brought to America from Europe by the Kroons!

"Would you mind describing this Mr Jones to me?" Nancy asked.

Mrs Ayres's description fitted Reinhold Kroon. The pieces of the puzzle were falling together fast!

"Did Lola Flanders bring any jewellery with her?" Nancy wanted to know.

Mrs Ayres looked startled at the question. It was fully a minute before she replied. During the interim, Nancy wondered what was going through the woman's mind. Had she been intimidated by Kroon, or was she, too, a partner in the mystery?

"Mr Jones," the woman began haltingly, "he's rather slow paying. He never sends cheques but comes here about once a year with the money. But three years ago he didn't turn up until very late. I couldn't keep Lola here for nothing—you know how it is," she said apologetically.

Nancy nodded and urged the woman to go on with her story. Mrs Ayres said that when she had talked to Lola about what they could do, her patient had finally produced a very beautiful bracelet which she had secreted in her luggage.

"Lola and I took a little trip to London to pawn it," she said. "I told her she'd better not use her right name, because the police sometimes get after these pawnshop dealers and she might get in trouble."

"So she used the name of Laura Flynn, didn't she?" Nancy asked.

Mrs Ayres almost toppled from her chair in surprise. Nancy told her not to be worried—that she had received that very bracelet as a gift and had been trying ever since to find out who the original owner was.

"How long has Mrs Flanders been an amnesia victim?" she asked.

Mrs Ayres replied that it was ever since Lola had come to live with her. She was not a victim of complete amnesia—it was more a case of forgetfulness and absent-mindedness than not knowing who she was.

"Every so often she seems to remember things very well," said Mrs Ayres. "But then her memory fades and for a long period she'll be almost like a child." Mrs Ayres leaned towards Nancy. "It's almost as though she were afraid the walls would pick up her words. To tell you the truth, Miss Drew, I think maybe the medicine Lola gets has something to do with it."

"She's under a doctor's care?" Nancy questioned.

Mrs Ayres nodded and said that the physician was not a local man. He came out a couple of times a year from London to see the ex-circus performer. He left a large supply of some white powder which Lola was to take every third day.

Nancy said the woman was no doubt right in her supposition about the medicine.

"It's all right for me to see Mrs Flanders, isn't it?"

Once more, Mrs Ayres seemed undecided as to what she should do. But finally she made up her mind.

Nancy's pulse quickened as she followed the woman up a narrow, winding stairway. Mrs Ayres opened one of the bedroom doors and called out:

"Lola, you have a visitor from the United States."

As Nancy walked in, she saw a sweet grey-haired woman seated in an old-fashioned rocker. At once there was no doubt in Nancy's mind that she was looking at Lolita Flanders' mother!

"How do you do, Mrs Flanders," she said, going forward and shaking hands with the woman. "I've come a long way to see you. How are you feeling?"

"It is very nice to meet you, my dear," Mrs Flanders said. "I never have any visitors."

Nancy told her that one of her former friends lived not far away. He had seen her at a circus not long before and had tried to speak to her. "But you left rather quickly," said Nancy.

Mrs Flanders turned searching eyes on Mrs Ayres. Apparently she did not remember the incident.

"Oh, yes, we went to the circus when it came here," said Mrs Ayres. "Who is this person you speak of?"

"His name is Pietro," said Nancy, watching Lolita's mother closely.

Mrs Flanders jumped from her chair. For a few seconds the cloudiness in her eyes seemed to disappear completely.

"Pietro!" she cried excitedly. "How well I remember him! One of the best clowns the circus ever had."

Nancy was thrilled to hear Mrs Flanders reminisce. But suddenly the woman's face seemed to cloud over.

"What was it you were asking me, my dear?" she said sweetly.

Mrs Ayres shrugged as if to say, "You see how it is?"

But Nancy was not discouraged. She felt sure that with the right kind of care Lola Flanders' memory might be restored completely.

"I haven't told you," said Nancy, "but I'm a friend of your daughter Lolita."

"Lolita?" Mrs Flanders frowned, as if she were trying very hard to recall the name.

"Lolita is with Sims' Circus now," Nancy went on. "She's one of the most brilliant aerialists in the United States."

"Little Lolita," Mrs Flanders said, hardly audibly. "My little Lolita. She died when she was very young."

Nancy was shocked. Apparently Mrs Flanders had been told that her child was no longer living. Another one of Kroon's tricks!

Nancy decided not to pursue this subject. It might bring painful memories to the girl's mother.

Instead she said, "Mrs Flanders, a queen once gave you a beautiful bracelet with horse charms, didn't she?"

Again Lola Flanders rose from her chair, and her eyes flashed.

"Yes," she said excitedly. "Mrs Ayres, where is my bracelet?"

Nancy motioned the woman not to reply. Pulling up her coat sleeve, Nancy said:

"Mrs Flanders, is this your bracelet?"

Mrs Flanders stared at the piece of jewellery as if she were seeing a ghost. Nancy removed the bracelet and put it on Lola Flanders' thin wrist.

As the woman stared at it, all the unnaturalness about her seemed to disappear. She straightened up, lifted her chin, and smiled at Nancy and Mrs Ayres.

"Please tell me more about this bracelet. You say it is yours, Miss Drew. How did you get it?"

Nancy decided to make the story brief.

"It came from a shop in the States," she said. "An aunt of mine saw it and bought it for me."

Lola Flanders nodded, and Nancy hurried on with her task of awakening the woman's mind completely. Putting an arm about her, she said:

"You have thought so many years that your lovely little girl was no longer living. This isn't true. Lolita is alive and well. She lives in the United States. She's one of the most beautiful girls I've ever seen."

On the spur of the moment, Nancy decided not to mention again that she was an aerialist. It might recall Lola's accident to her and have a disastrous effect on her mind.

"My little girl is alive?" Lola Flanders exclaimed happily.

Nancy nodded. "How would you like to see her?" she asked.

This question almost overpowered Lola Flanders. She looked at Mrs Ayres as if it were necessary to obtain her permission.

The woman smiled and came forward. Taking hold of Lola Flanders' hand, she said:

"This is wonderful news, isn't it? I think you should go and see your daughter."

Nancy now told the women that her father, who was a lawyer, was outside waiting for her. He could arrange the legal steps so that Lola Flanders might accompany them back to the States very soon. Nancy also went on to say that Pietro and his son were waiting with her father.

"Oh, I want to see them!" Lola Flanders said.

Suddenly she looked at her shabby clothes. Then she shook her head. Speaking like an old trouper, she told the others that she could not possibly appear in public until she had something done with her hair and she had a pretty new gown. Nancy and Mrs Ayres laughed. For the next few moments they helped Lola Flanders array herself as she wished. Nancy helped comb her hair in a more modern and becoming style. From a closet Mrs Ayres brought out her own best dress. She wore it only to church, she said.

"Put this on," Mrs Ayres insisted.

Lola Flanders slipped it over her head, and giggling as happily as a girl, she surveyed herself in the mirror.

When she was ready, the former circus performer went downstairs. Nancy hurried outside and brought the men in.

"Lola! Lola! This is wonderful!" the elder Pietro cried, kissing her.

Mrs Flanders blushed. Then Nancy introduced her father and the younger Pietro.

"How soon could Mrs Flanders be ready to leave?" Nancy asked Mrs Ayres.

"Any time," the owner of the nursing home said. "She has very little in the way of baggage. It wouldn't take ten minutes to pack it."

Before Lola Flanders knew what was happening, she and her suitcase were in the big automobile, and she was saying goodbye to Mrs Ayres, promising to write to her often and tell her what was happening.

The trip back to London did not take long. By the following morning, Mr Drew had made arrangements for taking Lola Flanders back to the States. He and Nancy had decided not to cable Lolita. While they hoped Mrs Flanders would not have a relapse, they agreed that it would be better to wait until they arrived home before telling Lolita the wonderful news.

At the airport the Pietros said goodbye. The younger clown took Nancy aside and asked if she would let him know when it might be feasible for him to return to the States.

"Do you think I should tell Mrs Flanders that Lolita and I are going to be married?"

"Not yet," Nancy replied. "There are a lot of things to be done before the mystery is completely solved."

As the travellers boarded the plane, Lola Flanders clung to Nancy. It had been a long time since she had made a trip across the ocean and never by plane. But the journey was a smooth and happy one.

When they landed in New York, a messenger delivered several telegrams to the plane. The stewardess handed one of them to Nancy.

Quickly she tore it open, then stared at the sheet in horror. The message had been sent by Bess from River Heights and read:

LOLITA BADLY INJURED. WILL MEET YOU HOTEL COLES NEW YORK WITH DETAILS.

23

Dodging Spies

For a few moments Nancy sat in stunned silence. Then quickly she showed the telegram to her father, and in a whisper cautioned him not to read it aloud.

"Mrs Flanders mustn't see it," she said hurriedly.

Trying not to show her agitation, Nancy helped Mrs Flanders from the plane. The woman looked around in a dazed fashion. For a moment Nancy was fearful that Mrs Flanders might suffer a mental relapse. But suddenly the ex-circus performer smiled and said:

"To think that I am back in the U.S.A.! Oh, it doesn't seem possible that in a little while I'll see my daughter again!"

"We'll have to find out where she is," said Nancy gently. "I don't know where the circus is right now."

She led Mrs Flanders to the women's lounge and asked the matron if she would please look after her for a few minutes. The kindly woman promised to do so.

Nancy hurried off to find her father. At the baggage desk, she said to him in a low voice:

"Dad, I've just come to the conclusion that the telegram is a hoax. Nobody in the States knew when we were flying back."

"It's just possible," said Mr Drew, "that the doctor who attended Lola Flanders may have visited the nursing home and found out that she had left for the States. He could have cabled Kroon."

Nancy decided that the only way to settle the matter was to call Bess's home. Going at once to the telephone booth, she placed the call. Bess herself answered.

"Where are you?" she asked Nancy.

"New York City. I just landed. Bess, did you send me a telegram?"

"Why, no," Bess replied in surprise. "What made you think I had?"

Nancy told her that someone had signed her name to a very unfortunate message. Then she asked if Bess had heard from Lolita recently.

"Why, yes. I just spoke to Erika. Lolita is fine. Why do you want to know?"

Nancy told her about the latest developments. Bess gasped, first in horror that anyone could be so cruel as to send such a message, and then in delight to hear that Lolita's mother had been found.

"Where is the circus playing?" Nancy asked.

"It's moving to Melville tonight. They'll be there for three days. That's why Erika called me. She wanted to know if there was any news of Pietro."

Quickly Nancy gave Bess the other details of the trip and concluded by saying that Pietro wanted to return to the circus as soon as possible and marry Lolita.

"When Erika calls again, will you please give Lolita his message."

Returning to her father, who had just received their baggage, Nancy told him the latest turn of events. Mr Drew became grave.

"One thing is sure. We are being spied upon. We'll have to be very careful."

He went to get a taxi and Nancy hurried to the women's lounge for Lola Flanders.

When they arrived at Eloise Drew's apartment, the

lawyer took his sister aside to ask if Lola Flanders might stay at her apartment temporarily. Under the circumstances, it seemed best to keep her in hiding until the riddle of the strange telegram had been solved.

Eloise Drew was delighted with the arrangement. Nancy was to stay there also. Mr Drew said that he had to return to his office at once and would catch an afternoon plane to River Heights.

After luncheon, Nancy said she would like to do an errand. Actually she wanted to talk to Captain Smith and tell him what she had found out in England. Miss Drew also said that she had an errand which must be taken care of.

"Do you mind staying alone?" Nancy asked Mrs Flanders.

The woman laughed. It was the first time Nancy had heard her laugh and it reassured the girl as to Lola Flanders' condition.

"Go ahead," Mrs Flanders said. "You know, I feel like a new person. I have no more fears."

Nancy and her aunt left the apartment together. Miss Drew said that she would not be gone more than twenty minutes, and Nancy could take all the time she needed. They separated, and Nancy went at once to call on Captain Smith.

"You back so soon?" the officer shook his head. "Well, what's the news?"

After hearing Nancy's story, Captain Smith looked at her in admiration. He said no detective or police officer could have done the job better and probably not so fast.

"There's still a great deal to be done," Nancy said. "Have you found out any more about the Tristam Booking Agency or Lola Flanders' dividend cheques?"

"I have some news that will amaze you," the officer

said. "The Tristam Booking Agency has gone out of business!"

"It has?" Nancy exclaimed.

The police officer said that the firm had folded up overnight. It had left no forwarding address.

"There has been no mail for Lola Flanders for two days," the captain stated. "I was just about to telephone one of the companies from which the dividend checks come to find out if they had been notified of any change of address. I'll do it now."

He put in a call to an oil company. Presently he received the information he wanted. Hanging up, he turned to Nancy and said:

"Well, that's a break. The new address is the Hotel Coles in this city!"

Before Nancy could do any more than show her surprise, the captain was placing another call. This time it was to the hotel desk. He learned that a young dancer named Lola Flanders had registered there the day before.

Nancy told Captain Smith about the fake telegram, directing her to go to the Hotel Coles.

"But you didn't do it?" the man asked, a look of disapproval crossing his face.

"No."

"I'm glad," the officer said. "It's a low-class place."

Captain Smith said he would send a detective to the hotel at once to check on Lola Flanders. He would have another man check to find out who had sent the telegram.

"Please call me at my aunt's home if you find out anything," Nancy requested.

The officer promised to do so and Nancy returned to the Drew apartment. She rang the bell and instantly the door was opened by her Aunt Eloise. The woman's eyes had a frightened look in them.

"Nancy! Lola Flanders is gone!" she cried.

· 24 ·

Terror at the Circus

Miss Eloise Drew began pacing the floor. She was convinced that Lola Flanders had suffered another attack of amnesia and wandered off.

Nancy was even more alarmed than her aunt. She was fearful that one of her enemies had enticed Mrs Flanders away.

Hastening to the street, she asked a group of children she saw playing there if they had seen a woman come from the apartment house.

"A thin, small woman with greying hair," she added.

"Sure I saw her," a little girl spoke up. "She got in a taxi and went off."

"Was anybody with her?" Nancy asked.

The little girl said that a woman with curly blond hair and very red cheeks had come from the apartment house with the woman and they had gone off together.

"Did you happen to hear them say where they were going?"

"No, I didn't," the child replied.

Nancy's first thought was the Hotel Coles. She wanted to go there at once, but recalling Captain Smith's advice, decided to phone him and ask the police to make the investigation.

A few moments later the police captain called and reported that the young dancer who called herself Lola Flanders had not been at the hotel since she had registered.

Suddenly an idea occurred to Nancy. Consulting the classified telephone directory, she made a series of calls to theatre booking agents and restaurants that employed dancers. The list was long and she was kept busy for an hour and a half. At last she was rewarded, however. Millie Francine was employed at the Bon Ton Night Club.

Nancy wondered how she could get in touch with the dancer. Even if she knew nothing about Lolita's mother and her possible kidnapping, she might be able to give her a lead to the guilty party.

As the girl detective sat thinking, the bell rang. She ran to the door, hopeful that Lola Flanders had returned. Ned Nickerson stood there, grinning.

"I know you didn't expect me," he said, stepping into the apartment. "I hadn't left New York yet, and when I telephoned earlier to find out if by any chance you were back, I was certainly delighted to hear that you had returned. So here I am!"

Nancy stared at him in surprise. The strange look on her face made Ned ask:

"Aren't you glad to see me?"

"Oh, yes, Ned," Nancy said hurriedly. "But we're in the middle of a new mystery. Who answered the phone here when you called?"

"I don't know. Whoever she was told me that you

and your aunt had gone out for a few hours."

"Ned, that was Lolita Flanders' mother! At least, I think it was," she said, upon second thought. "What else did she say?"

"That if I wanted to see you, not to come for a while, because nobody would be here."

"She said that?" Nancy asked in surprise. "Go on, Ned," she urged.

"There isn't any more to tell. Well, wait a minute," he said suddenly. "It seems to me she did say that she was going out, too."

"Did she say why?" Nancy asked quickly.

Ned said the woman had mumbled something. It could have been that she was going to meet her daughter.

"Oh, Ned," said Nancy, "it's just as I feared. Lola Flanders has been kidnapped!"

"What do you mean?" he asked.

Nancy told him the whole story and then said, "Ned, you and I are going to the Bon Ton as fast as we can get there."

"Well, I'm glad to have a date," Ned said. "But would you mind telling me why you've picked out that second-rate place? Besides, it doesn't open until evening."

Nancy was disappointed. Valuable hours would be lost in her search for Lola Flanders. Presently she said hopefully, "Ned, often the girls who perform in those places have afternoon rehearsals. Let's go over there, anyway."

To Nancy's delight, there was no doorman on duty and the Bon Ton was open. As she had predicted, a rehearsal was going on. She sat down at a table in an obscure, dark corner and watched.

It was not difficult to identify Millie Francine because presently a director called out, "Millie, what's the matter with you? Your voice sounds as if you'd been eating gravel!"

Millie Francine proved to be a better dancer than singer, but she was nervous, and when her part in the show was over she sat down at a table not far from where Nancy and Ned were seated. They rose and went over to sit beside her. Looking straight into the dancer's eyes, Nancy asked in a low tone:

"Where have you hidden the real Lola Flanders?"

Millie Francine fell back as if someone had struck her. It was several seconds before she recovered her wits, then she asked who Nancy was.

"I'm a detective and I know all about you," Nancy replied. She gave the girl enough of the story to convince her.

Millie Francine had begun to shake with fright. She declared she was an innocent party.

"I used to work for Sims' Circus," she said. "Mr Kroon knew I needed money. When he suggested that I could earn some extra cash by pretending my real name was Lola Flanders, I said I would."

Millie Francine said she had been paid well by Kroon and Mr Tristam, the owner of the agency.

"I didn't see any harm in the pretence," the dancer said.

"But what about the mail that came to you in care of the agency?" Nancy asked.

Millie Francine's eyebrows went up. She said she had never received any mail there. Nancy now told her about the dividend cheques and her suspicion that Kroon and possibly Tristam were stealing them.

Nancy asked if Millie knew where the Tristams lived.

She gave them an apartment-house address and said that perhaps Lola Flanders was there. But Nancy had already thought of this.

"How soon will the rehearsal be over?" Nancy asked the dancer abruptly.

"I'm all through now," the girl replied.

"In that case, I'll go to your dressing-room and wait while you change. Then you're going with us to the apartment."

Twenty minutes later the three set off in a cab. Unbeknown to Nancy, Ned had telephoned Captain Smith and asked that a policeman meet them at the apartment house. Upon their arrival, they found him waiting.

Nancy suggested that Millie Francine call up to the apartment that she was there, but not to mention that she had other visitors with her. The dancer did her part and the front door was opened to them.

They went up in the elevator to the second floor and made their way to the Tristam apartment. Millie rang the bell. The door was opened by a woman with curly blonde hair whom the dancer called Mrs Tristam. The four callers burst in.

"What does this mean?" Mrs Tristam cried.

While the policeman stood guard at the door, Nancy and Ned hurried inside to look for Lola Flanders. They found her in the living-room, talking to Mr Tristam.

"Oh, Nancy!" Lolita's mother cried out. "It was dreadful of me not to have left a note. These kind people got in touch with me and we were going to leave in a few minutes to see my daughter."

"Mrs Flanders," said Nancy, "these people are not kind. They have practically kidnapped you. They have been stealing your money for years. They never intended to take you to Lolita."

As Lola Flanders fell back, stunned, Mr Tristam walked forward. He demanded to know what this outrageous story was all about and who Nancy was.

"I'm quite sure you know who I am," she said. "Possibly you do not know my escort, Ned Nickerson. And in case you do not know the policeman at the door, I suggest that you meet him quietly."

Suddenly Tristam's eyes blazed and he became virtually a madman. He shoved Nancy aside and punched Ned. Then he started for the door to the hall.

Before he could even reach the policeman, Millie Francine planted herself in his path.

"Oh, no, you don't, Mr Tristam," she cried. "You don't go another step without telling these people I'm innocent!"

At that moment there was a tap on the door. The policeman recognized it as a signal from more of Captain Smith's men. He opened the door. The officer and two other men walked in.

Tristam, seeing that the game was up, quietly surrendered. He told the story much as Nancy had pieced it together from time to time. He added that it was Kroon's idea when Lola Flanders, then a widow, was discharged from the hospital, to keep her under the influence of drugs so that she would appear to be an amnesia victim, and to place her in a cheap nursing home. It was Mrs Kroon who had literally abducted Lolita, partly because she had loved the little girl and partly because she knew that the aerialist had great talent and would bring a small fortune to them.

Nancy was fearful that the excitement might prove

disastrous to Lola Flanders' mind, but she seemed to have recovered completely. When she reached Aunt Eloise's apartment, she asked how soon they might start for Melville and see Lolita.

"If you feel well enough, we'll take the first plane," Nancy promised her.

"I'm ready to go now," she insisted.

Ned obtained the reservations and within two hours they were all saying goodbye to Aunt Eloise and setting off for the town of Melville.

As they climbed into the plane, the first person they saw was young Pietro! He explained that he had just arrived from England.

"I just couldn't stay away," he said. "Nancy, I had a hunch you would fix everything up, and that it won't be long before Lolita and I will be married."

"I think you're right," Nancy said, smiling at Ned, "and Lolita will have her wish—that her mother will be present at the wedding."

The plane reached Melville just before midnight. The group went to the hotel. Nancy suggested that Lola Flanders remain there until Lolita could be brought to her.

"I don't know whether Mr Kroon has been apprehended yet or not," Nancy said. Turning to Ned and Pietro, she added, "Suppose we three go over to the circus at five o'clock tomorrow morning and mingle with the crowd that will be watching the workmen set up the tents. In that way, we won't be noticed by Mr or Mrs Kroon or any of their spies. We'll get Lolita and bring her back here."

This plan was agreed upon. Nancy was up at four thirty the next morning, and at five set off with the young men. Upon reaching the circus grounds, the three separated, Nancy going ahead. She made her way carefully to Lolita's trailer and knocked.

"Lolita, wake up!"

Sleepily the young aerialist tumbled out of bed and opened the door. Seeing Nancy, she started to cry out.

"*Sh-h-h!*" Nancy warned her. "Your mother is in a hotel down town. Dress quietly and follow me."

Lolita dressed quickly, and throwing caution to the winds, stepped out of her trailer.

"Oh, Nancy, this is marvellous! Let's hurry."

The two girls made their way along, hurrying past the wild-animal cages to avoid detection by Kroon, should he happen to be around. But they did not see him, and hastened on happily.

They had just reached King Kat's cage when a strong hand was suddenly laid on Nancy's shoulder. The person gripped her tightly and swung her about.

Kroon!

"So you're still trying to thwart me!" the man cried. "Well, this is the last time!"

With his free hand, he unfastened the lion's cage and thrust Nancy forward!

· 25 ·

Last Links in the Mystery

WITH a great leap the huge lion sprang towards the door of the cage. Nancy Drew fought with every ounce of strength to get away from the insane ringmaster who was pushing her into the cage. Lolita screamed and tried to pull her foster father away.

A few yards behind Nancy was Ned Nickerson. And a short distance behind him, Pietro. Both young men raced forward.

Ned grasped Nancy and swung her away from the lion. The angry, confused beast landed one claw on the boy's hand and raked it badly.

Ned's action had startled Kroon, who fell backwards. The lion hesitated a moment as though undecided whether to slink away or jump forward. For a fearful second everyone wondered whether the beast would get loose.

Pietro saw a long whip lying on the ground. Quick as a flash he picked it up and cracked it across King Kat's nose. The lion snarled and bared its teeth. One paw, halfway through the opening, was keeping Pietro from closing the cage door. With another crack of the whip he struck the lion's paw and the beast jumped backward with a roar of pain. The clown slammed and locked the door.

By this time there was terrific commotion in the

circus. Every workman and many of the townspeople had come on the run to see what had happened. In the mêlée, Kroon disappeared.

"Oh, Nancy!" Lolita cried. "Are you all right?"

Nancy nodded. Recovering from her shock, she saw that Ned's hand was bleeding profusely.

"Ned!" she said quickly. "You must go to Dr Jackson at once!"

Then, realizing that she had not thanked him for his brave rescue, she added, "Ned, you saved my life. How can I ever thank you?"

Ned gave a wry smile. "Don't even try, Nancy. I'm only thankful I was here to do it."

Pietro, too, came in for his share of praise.

Quickly Nancy looked around. "Where did Mr Kroon go?" she asked.

No one had noticed him leave. Nancy, fearful that he would escape, asked Lolita to take Ned to the doctor.

"Pietro," she said, "we must find Mr Kroon."

The man was not on the circus grounds and Mrs Kroon also was missing. Pietro reported that the ringmaster's car was gone. Nancy telephoned State Police headquarters and spoke to the sergeant on duty. She was told that the police had just received word from New York to apprehend Kroon and were about to pick him up at the circus.

"Thank you, Miss Drew," the sergeant said. "I'll send a detail out at once and we'll set up a road block."

The Kroons were picked up a short time later on the highway and taken to headquarters. Nancy, Lolita, Pietro, and Ned were present at the interrogation.

Kroon, finding that denials of his crooked schemes were futile, and that even his two spies, the tramp clown and the giant, had not been entirely loyal to him, made a full confession. He did not spare the Tristams, on whom he put a great deal of the blame. At Kroon's request, Tristam had come to River Heights and stolen the horse-charm bracelet. He had brought it to Kroon, who years before had had a cheap duplicate of Lolita's horse charm made. He had kept the original, hoping to obtain the valuable bracelet. He had finally succeeded.

But when Nancy had stymied his plan to sell it, Kroon and Tristam together had engineered the kidnapping of Nancy and George. Learning that this had failed, Tristam had found out where Nancy had gone and followed her to New York. He had tried to stop Nancy's trip to England by engaging a professional thug to put the acid in her overnight bag.

While Kroon and Tristam had managed to steal the dividend cheques which had come to Lola Flanders from her securities, they had never dared to try selling the securities themselves. Lolita was thrilled to hear that they were still intact for her mother.

When Kroon finished his confession, the police asked Nancy and the others if they had any questions. The girl detective spoke up.

"I have just one," she said. "Mr Kroon, who was it who went to the riding academy and attacked Señor Roberto?"

The ringmaster said Tristam had done this also. Both he and Kroon felt that Hitch was in the way. Tristam had meant to attack the stableman, but had, in the semidarkness, mistaken Roberto for him. Just as he had discovered his error, Tristam heard voices in the distance and fled.

After all the angles of the mystery were cleared up, Nancy and her friends went at once to the Melville Hotel. Nancy suggested that no one attend the reunion of mother and daughter. Lolita smiled and thanked Nancy for being so understanding, but said that she wanted all of the others to come to her mother's room in fifteen minutes.

When Nancy and the young men arrived, they were thrilled to see the happiness on the faces of Lola and Lolita Flanders. Their praise of Nancy was boundless, and Ned and Pietro came in for their share.

"Mother and I have been talking over my wedding plans," said Lolita, blushing a little. "Mother has a wonderful idea."

The others listened eagerly as the pretty aerialist went on to say that Mrs Flanders would like the wedding to take place soon—three days from then.

"This is partly because she wants her daughter and her new son-in-law in business with her," Lolita explained.

Pietro looked puzzled. "In business?" he asked.

"Yes," said Lola Flanders, taking hold of the young clown's hand. "I had a telephone call a little while ago from Nancy's Aunt Eloise. The New York police have discovered that Sims' Circus is a stock company and I own most of the stock."

"Oh, that's perfectly wonderful," Nancy said, delighted.

Pietro asked how Sims figured in the deal. Lola Flanders told him that at one period, when the circus was about to fold up, Lolita's father had bought the major portion of the stock. Kroon knew this and kept reminding young Mr Sims of the fact whenever he stayed around the circus too long.

The ringmaster had confidentially told him that it was still a mystery as to whether Lola Flanders was alive. Some day she might show up and claim her rightful share. Since young Sims knew little about the running of a circus, he had gladly left this to the stronger-willed Kroon.

Pietro suddenly kissed his future mother-in-law. Then he said, "Bad as Mr Kroon was, I certainly have him to thank for one thing. Sims' is still a fine circus."

"Indeed it is," said Lolita. "Mother, wait until you see a performance."

Nancy asked what had happened to the Vascon troupe. Lolita said that when Rosa had been unable to perform, Mr Kroon had discharged the whole equestrian troupe. Suddenly Lolita looked at Nancy.

"Oh," she said, "it would be so wonderful if they would come back and we could have a full performance the night of the wedding. Nancy, would you ride in Rosa's place?"

The girl detective smiled and said she would be very happy to take part in the act.

On the night of the gala performance Nancy's family and friends sat in Box AA, with Senor Roberto, who had fully recovered from his injuries. Bess whispered to George:

"This is so marvellous I could cry. It's the best mystery Nancy ever solved."

"It was swell," George agreed. "But you just wait. Another good mystery will come Nancy's way and I'll bet it won't be long, either."

George was right! Nancy had hardly recovered from her days at the circus when she was confronted with another mystery, which would become known as *Nancy's Mysterious Letter*.

During the evening, it seemed as though each performer outdid himself. Nancy herself felt as if she had never done her stunt riding so well. The wedding plans had been announced to the audience, and after the finale, everyone stayed in his seat.

The happy bride and her real prince were married in the great ring. Then, as they walked out together smiling, to the tune of the Mendelsohn march, the applause was thunderous.

A reception had been arranged in the cafeteria tent. In one corner on a large table the wedding gifts were displayed. Prominent among them was the picture of Nancy Drew, standing on a horse in her circus costume. Lola Flanders had asked Eloise Drew for it. A little later the radiant bride said to Nancy:

"This will be a constant reminder of the most wonderful girl I have ever met!"

Then Lolita held up her arm on which she was wearing the beautiful horse-charm bracelet.

"Are you sure you want me to have this as a wedding gift?" she asked Nancy.

"Of course I do," Nancy replied. "The bracelet came from a queen and now it has come back to one—the queen of aerialists!"

The Hardy Boys Mystery Stories

by FRANKLIN W. DIXON

Look out for these thrilling new mysteries which will be coming soon in Armada.

The Mystery of Smugglers Cove (62)

When a valuable painting is stolen, the Hardy Boys are determined to catch the thieves. But the trail of clues soon leads them to the steamy swamps of Florida – and to a deadly encounter with some man-eating alligators!

The Stone Idol (63)

The strange disappearance of an ancient stone statue begins a hair-raising new adventure for the Hardys. But their investigations lead them into a sinister trap – in the freezing wilderness of the Antarctic.